"Why hasn't anyone tied you down?

"Since you are that most elusive creature—young, handsome, single, successful."

"I'm more cautious since starting my own business," he replied. "I've learned to take calculated risks."

"Really?"

They locked eyes. Jackson nodded. "I need... something."

"Collateral?"

"Skin in the game."

She swirled the wine in the glass. "I didn't peg you for one to play it safe."

"Not safe," he said. "Smart."

Jackson wanted something from her, some reassurance that she would take him seriously. If it didn't work out between them, fine. He could live with that. But it wouldn't be because they hadn't tried.

Alexa returned her attention to the chessboard. For a long while, she sat still, calculating her next move. Whether it was with the match or with him, he wasn't quite sure.

* * *

Rivalry at Play by Nadine Gonzalez is part of the Texas Cattleman's Club: Ranchers and Rivals series.

Dear Reader,

Consider this your membership to the exclusive Texas Cattleman's Club! While sipping cocktails at the event of the summer, keep an eye out for Alexandra Lattimore and Jackson Strom, who are reconnecting after years apart. Alexa and Jackson would have been high school sweethearts if only they had quit one-upping each other. This unexpected run-in sparks the rivalry anew. Tell all your friends about it.

For more about me, visit my website, www.nadine-gonzalez.com.

For a quick trip to Miami, Florida, without ever leaving the house, check out my latest Harlequin Desire releases, *Scandal in the VIP Suite* and *What Happens in Miami...*

To lasting love!

Nadine

NADINE GONZALEZ

RIVALRY AT PLAY

HARLEQUIN
DESIRE

Special thanks and acknowledgment are given to
Nadine Gonzalez for her contribution to the
Texas Cattleman's Club: Ranchers and Rivals miniseries.

Recycling programs
for this product may
not exist in your area.

ISBN-13: 978-1-335-58126-6

Rivalry at Play

Harlequin Enterprises ULC
22 Adelaide St. West, 40th Floor
Toronto, Ontario M5H 4E3, Canada
www.Harlequin.com

Printed in U.S.A.

Nadine Gonzalez is a Haitian American author. A lawyer by profession, she lives in Miami, Florida, and shares her home with her Cuban American husband and their son.

Nadine writes joyous contemporary romance featuring a diverse cast of characters, American, Caribbean and Latinx. She networks on Twitter but lives on Instagram and increasingly on TikTok! Check out @_nadinegonzalez.

For more information, visit her website, nadine-gonzalez.com.

Books by Nadine Gonzalez

Harlequin Desire

Miami Famous

Scandal in the VIP Suite
What Happens in Miami...

Texas Cattleman's Club

The Rebel's Return
Rivalry at Play

Visit her Author Profile page at Harlequin.com, or nadine-gonzalez.com, for more titles.

You can also find Nadine Gonzalez on Facebook, along with other Harlequin Desire authors, at Facebook.com/harlequindesireauthors.

For Ariel and Nathaniel. Always.

One

"A bottle of Prosecco for Ms. Alexandra Lattimore."

"On the table, please."

"Very well, Miss."

The poolside attendant's voice had roused Alexa from a heat-induced slumber. It had that sweet, syrupy drawl that might have charmed her—if she were easily charmed. She yawned and stretched and felt around for her tote bag. The August heat was relentless. A bottle of water might have been a smarter choice, but she needed something light and bubbly to lift her mood. She'd only been back in her hometown a few days, and already she had to attend a country club fundraiser. Such was life in Royal, Texas. In a move that fooled no one, her mother had purchased the admission ticket, feigned a migraine and insisted Alexa attend in her place. But that didn't mean she couldn't do things her way: Prosecco, gelato, a couple of podcasts cued up on her phone and a cabana all to herself.

Upon learning of her plans, her sister, Caitlyn, had chastised her for dropping five hundred dollars on a glorified tent.

"It's for charity," Alexa said in her defense. "It's the right thing to do."

Caitlyn accused her of being antisocial. "Everyone will be there. It's a great opportunity to connect with old friends or make new ones. Every time you've come home, you've stayed here at the ranch unless we've dragged you out. Don't wall yourself off. You just never know."

It was the sort of bland advice that people in love doled out to anyone who'd listen. Caitlyn—who would swan dive into the pool party on the arm of her new fiancé, flashing a smile brighter than her engagement ring—was sick and sloppy in love. Jonathan and Jayden, her single brothers, weren't coming until later, so she couldn't even hang out with them.

"Here's what I know," she'd replied. "If anyone wants to connect or reconnect with me, they'll have to put in the work and find me first."

Alexa was a prima donna of the highest order, and she was okay with it.

"What if you run into an old flame?"

"Please, Caitlyn," Alexa huffed. "I was seventeen when I left for college. The boys I knew couldn't start a flame with a box of matches and lighter fluid."

Even now, Alexa bristled at the thought. If she encountered an old flame, she'd stomp on it. No one had time for that.

Eyes still half-closed behind dark sunglasses, she

found her tote under her lounge chair, drew it onto her lap and rummaged for her money clip. "Wait a minute. I have something for you."

"No cash. A smile will do."

Oh? So the Texas Cattleman's Club attendants were cheeky now. That was new. She'd been away from home awhile, but customer service at the country club had always been world class.

Alexa slid her sunglasses down the length of her nose with the tip of her index finger. She expected to lock eyes with a cocky college student, some kid picking up shifts at the club over the summer. The man towering over her was no kid: tall, Black and built, in a fitted white tee and swim trunks. He had just enough facial hair to define his jaw and draw attention to a teasing smile.

Wait… Oh, God…wait! Oh, God… *No!*

Alexa's mind whirled through the seven stages of disbelief before finally rolling to a stop. A name slipped from her lips. "Jackson Strom."

His smile widened. "At your service."

Caitlyn had had it right. Just about *everyone* was here. "I haven't seen you since…"

"High school," he supplied.

"Sure."

Actually, the last time she'd laid eyes on him was the day after graduation, in the parking lot of a convenience store. She was on her way in, and he was heading to his car with a paper bag overflowing with snacks. She'd said "hi," he'd said "hey," and that was that.

One month later, she'd moved to New York City for college and law school. Presently, she lived in Miami and worked for a prestigious law firm. This wasn't her first time back in town. After years away, her recent trips had started in May for the funeral of a lifelong neighbor and family friend. But her visits were short and, for the most part, she stuck close to home. Alexa wouldn't admit this to anyone, but she'd broken into a cold sweat at the thought of coming to the Texas Cattleman's Club—the beating heart of Royal's society—alone, hence the cabana.

Jackson welcomed her back in town.

"Thanks. Are you the official welcome wagon?"

"Kind of, but they only trot me out for very important people."

"I'm flattered."

"I'm flattered you remember my name."

"How could I forget? It was listed second in rank to mine everywhere."

He cut her a glance. The mischievous look confirmed that the boy she once knew and the man before her now were one and the same. His appearance had thrown her off. Her old high school nemesis had looked nothing like this. He'd been good-looking then. Lanky and all limbs, he played basketball. The girls liked him, but "cute" was the word often used to describe him. All that cuteness had burned away in ten years. Jackson was handsome. His youthful cockiness had been honed into confidence. And yet he still had a dimple in his left cheek. The well-trimmed beard didn't hide it.

"What brings you back to Royal, Alexa?"

"I'm handling a matter for my family."

That was an excessively watered-down version of the truth. The "matter" was a complex legal issue regarding the family ranch's oil rights. They were fighting an aggressive claim brought forward by a local rancher. There was no way to drop that casually into conversation, so she'd deliberately kept her answer vague.

"Ever the dutiful daughter."

"Some things don't change."

She was a Lattimore, and Lattimores stuck together even if it drained them of their lifeblood.

Jackson took a good look around the cabana while she got a good look at him. Some things *had* changed. He had the toned, chiseled body of a professional athlete, but Alexa knew better than most that his best asset was and always would be his sharp mind. Jackson Strom had been the smartest boy in her class. Alexa had been the smartest—period.

"This is a nice setup," he said.

"I like it." The canvas-covered hideaway offered a respite from the August heat. At the same time, it offered a full view of the party. If anything important happened, she wouldn't miss it. Later, she'd have something to report to her mother, some bit of gossip to satisfy and please her, and all would be well. "Join me for a drink?"

"Call me boring," he said, already uncorking the bottle, "but on a hot day, I prefer a cold beer."

She squinted and studied him a moment. Who would ever call him boring? Back when they were just kids in school, he had always been the fun, easygoing one who got along with just about everyone. "We could order beer if you like."

"This'll do," he said. "Do you really think I'd pass on the chance to have a drink with Alexandra the First?"

Alexa flinched at the old nickname. Alexandra the First...at everything. Top of the class, best of the best, honorable mention, Dean's list, on and on. She'd been crowned the class intellectual snob. Like any label, it was unfair and unearned. She'd done nothing to deserve it except excel at everything but track and field. But every high school drama needed a villain, and she'd assumed the role. What was the alternative? Make nice and try to fit in? Never. She was the odd peg that didn't fit anywhere, not even with her own rock-solid nuclear family. While she read quietly in her room or immersed herself in foreign languages for hours, her siblings got their kicks fishing, hiking, horseback riding and swinging through any and all trees.

"That's 'Stuck-Up Queen Alexandra the First,' mind you," she said. "I dropped the title and go by Alexa now. It was a mouthful."

His laugh was rolling thunder. "You were always quick with a comeback."

"We all have our gifts."

He lifted the bottle of sparkling wine from the ice bucket and poured and filled two glasses. For a beer drinker, he had the moves of a master sommelier. He handed her a glass. "I spotted you in the lobby, but you breezed by."

She'd *sped* by everyone, avoiding eye contact. An attendant had directed her to the reserved cabana, and she'd been hiding out ever since. It didn't matter that she was an accomplished attorney. Here, she would forever be the odd one out.

"Sorry about that," she said breezily. "Have a seat."

He eyed the empty lounge chair next to hers. "Were you expecting anyone?"

"I wasn't expecting you, that's for sure."

Jackson set the bottle in the ice bucket and stretched out his long legs on the lounge chair. He had always moved like that, smooth and unhurried. "You were always good on your own, weren't you?"

"Not really."

She hadn't been a loner by choice. The girl who ranked first in academics often ranked dead last in everything that mattered, such as making friends or finding a date to prom.

He frowned. "Tell me more."

"Never mind. I've worked it all out with my therapist."

Whatever pedestal she had been placed on during high school, Jackson had been determined to knock her off it. For four years straight, they'd gone head-to-head for every medal, every prize, every scrap of recognition the education system had to offer. He tried his best, but he never outpaced her. But she often wondered why he'd been so intent on ruining her life. Being the best was all she'd had. Without that distinction, she was no one and had nothing to fall back on. It wasn't like she was going to take up cheerleading or join the glee club.

"You make it sound like it was a hardship. You left us all in the dust."

"Can you blame me?"

"Honestly? Yeah," he said. "You were the coolest girl in class. I would've killed to be your friend."

Alexa tossed her head back and laughed.

"What's so funny?"

"Excuse me." She stifled a giggle. "I find that hard to believe."

He took a long sip from his glass. "What was up with us?"

Now *that* was a loaded question. "It started sophomore year—"

"No," he said flatly. "It started way before that."

They'd been in the same class ever since kindergarten. Their rivalry hadn't begun in earnest until first semester sophomore year. Jackson had placed second at the local science fair. Usually, a girl named Stephanie Davies placed second in these types of competitions, but she had moved away. That day, Alexa saw Jackson with new eyes. She caught his cocky grin as he raised his smaller trophy over his stupid head. The urge to slap that grin off his face was irresistible.

"I can only speak for myself," Alexa said. "Our tenth-grade science fair kicked it off for me. I wanted to rip that trophy out of your hands."

Jackson settled more comfortably and bit into a smile. "Sounds hot. I would've liked that."

Suddenly, Alexa was hot. "Well, when do you think it started?"

"Eighth-grade chess tournament."

"What?"

"Ms. Thomson's math-class special project."

"I remember," she said, hazy on the details. Their math teacher had organized an in-class chess tournament as an extra-credit activity. Alexa had never played chess before then, but a few quick online tutorials had gotten her up to speed. She'd won, but... "I don't remember playing you."

"Not surprised. You wiped me out in twelve moves."

Maybe it was the heavy August heat or the light sparkling wine, but the past was soup. It took a while before she remembered. "Ah! You left your queen vulnerable. Who does that?"

"Not you, Queen Alexandra."

"Hmm." Outside the cocoon of the cabana, the party was picking up. Music and laughter and conversation tangled in a distracting mess. Alexa's mind went quiet. "It was you, wasn't it? You started the whole Queen Alexandra the First stuff."

Jackson took another sip from his glass. "I won't confirm or deny it."

"All this because of Ms. Thomson's extra-credit chess tournament?"

"I've wanted to beat you ever since."

"I'll take you up whenever."

Jackson flagged over a poolside attendant with whom he seemed pretty chummy and whom he'd likely bribed to confiscate her order from the bar. Instead of ordering a craft beer, he asked where he might find a chessboard.

"Right here." The attendant lifted the lid off a wicker basket tucked in a corner. It held a collection of board games, puzzles and toys for kids. "We have chess, checkers, Scrabble…"

"Chess, please."

He slipped the man a crisp twenty-dollar bill and set up the board on the round cocktail table between them.

Alexa sat up straight. "Are you serious? We're not playing chess at a pool party."

"Would you rather play volleyball?"

"I'd rather nap."

"You've got to give me a chance to redeem myself. It's the only way to save this budding friendship."

"Fine." It had been a while since she'd played chess. This might be his lucky day.

He arranged the white pawns nearest her. "Are you really here alone?"

"My siblings will show up at some point." Caitlyn was prancing about with Dev. Her brothers, Jonathan and Jayden, would swing by eventually.

"That's not what I meant." His focus was on the board, lining up the plastic pawns in neat rows. She wasn't fooled. He was waiting for an answer.

"Are you asking if I'm single?"

He glanced up. "Are you?"

"There's no ring on my finger."

"If there had been one, I would have gotten word. Whatever the Lattimores do is news."

"Only in Royal."

"Only Royal matters."

"I beg to differ. There's a big world out there."

"And I've seen most of it. It doesn't change the fact that I know where home is."

She admired his self-awareness. They were about the same age, twenty-eight. Most of their peers were scattered to the winds. But Jackson knew where he belonged, where best to plant roots and grow. She hadn't yet figured that out.

"And you're a lawyer in Miami?"

"That's right." Alexa took a healthy sip of Prosecco to ease down a ball of anxiety that had formed in her throat. She didn't want to talk about her job. "I guess everything we Lattimores do really is news."

"I told you."

"Is it my mother? Is she boring everyone to death with updates on my so-called adventures?"

"Your brothers, too."

"Damn it."

The board was set. He leaned back and folded his arms over his head. "Your move."

"Okay." Alexa took a sip of Prosecco. "Are *you* single?"

A slow smile drew out his lips. "That's not what I meant, but that's fine."

Alexa was burning hot again. Still, she fixed him with a cool gaze. "Just answer the question."

"I'm single. No rings. No commitments."

"That's catchy." She glanced down at the board and moved a rook. "You should get it in needlepoint."

Laughing, he reached over and advanced a pawn. "Alexa... I missed you."

He'd missed her because of her sharp tongue and not despite it. Interesting. What was even more interesting was that she'd missed him, too. It hadn't occurred to her until now. Alexa had actively erased her high school memories. She did not attend reunions or accept online friendship requests. Finally, she'd done her best to stomp out old flames. He fell into that last category. Like the other girls, she'd found him cute, very cute. He was the only boy to have held her attention—a good thing, too, because none of the others had spared her the time of day. Their rivalry had kept her on her toes. Honestly, it had kept her on the Dean's list right up until she graduated as valedictorian. It had probably gotten her into her dream school. Even so, Alexa hadn't thought for a minute that he'd seen her as anything other than a moving target.

"He likes you," a girl had pointed out one day after English class. Alexa had aced an oral presentation even though Jackson had raised his hand a dozen times to ask questions and poke holes in her argument. "Can't you tell?" Her classmate had delivered that last bit with a hair flip. The subtext was clear: the smartest girl in school wasn't necessarily the brightest. Alexa had laughed in her face. Now, though, she wondered. Meanwhile, she captured two of Jackson's pawns and a rook.

Two

Growing up, Jackson Strom had heard about the Lattimore legend. The clan was of solid Royal stock going several generations back. Augustus Lattimore had earned the title of patriarch by establishing the family ranch and running it for decades. He'd since passed the reins to Ben, his eldest son. Ben and wife, Barbara, had four children, including Alexandra. The one thing more intimidating than one Lattimore kid was all four of them clustered together. They roamed the earth as if descendants of titans. On a good day, Jonathan and Jayden were cool enough. The youngest daughter, Caitlyn, had always seemed shy. But Alexa *was* a queen, regal and elegant in all things. She was a beauty, too. Dark chestnut skin, coffee-black hair and the most incredible brown eyes fringed with thick lashes—all the better to look down her long nose at the world. One look from Alexa could turn a guy's insides into jelly. At least, that had been his experience, as far back as kindergarten.

She and Jackson had sat side by side throughout third grade. But he didn't think she noticed him—an attitude he reciprocated. Then came the eighth-grade chess tournament. Alexa beat him handily and dismissed him with a nod, as if he were nothing more than a waste of time. From that day, he made it his mission to beat her at something, anything. He failed. As he matured, he adjusted his goal. He tried gaining her respect and failed at that, too. By senior year, he set his sights on asking her out. The school year ended, and he'd never worked up the nerve.

He'd last laid eyes on her outside a convenience store. He'd said, "Hey," and kept it moving. Her valedictorian speech was still fresh in his mind. Crisp and concise, it had touched on the issues of the day and presented a realistic outlook for the future. Basically, it had put them all to shame. None of them could have come up with anything half as good. Had he known that was the last time he'd come in contact with her in a decade, he would've played it differently.

Since he'd seen her last, he'd enrolled in UT, met a girl, fallen in love, fallen out of love, moved on, earned his degree, started a business and been crowned with success. He'd kept tabs on her, though. Her family was eager to brag about her successes: law school, a job in a high-powered Manhattan firm and, recently, the move to Miami.

For the most part, Jackson was over his childish infatuation. Then she'd breezed past him in the lobby of the Texas Cattleman's Club, looking like a movie star with her hair sleeked back, dark glasses, bustier top and high-waisted shorts. As always, she'd brushed past him, her long, shapely legs taking long, purposeful strides. Jackson couldn't stomach it. This time, he would get her to notice him. The way she'd looked at him made him think he wouldn't have to work that hard. Now she was killing him at chess, and he truly didn't mind.

Caitlyn Lattimore stormed the cabana, trailed by a friend. She stopped abruptly, eyed their setup and declared, "Well, isn't this cozy?"

Alexa advanced a bishop. "You found me. Yoo-hoo."

"Checking in. That's all."

"You've checked in and I'm fine. Now run along."

Caitlyn plopped down beside her sister on the chaise. "Not a chance! Dev is playing volleyball, so I'm free for a while."

The friend stepped forward, whipped out her phone and snapped a photo. "Sorry, I had to document this," she said. "A-JACKS is back at it!"

"Wait. What?" Caitlyn screeched. Petite with long, wavy brown hair, a sandy-brown complexion and big brown eyes, she'd always been reserved. This was the most animated Jackson had ever seen her. She clutched a frozen margarita in one hand. It was more slush than anything else, but that could explain things.

Her friend filled her in. "These two were legends in high school, always competing for blue ribbons and dollar-store trophies and stuff."

Alexa kept her eyes on the board. "Blue ribbons? You make us sound like a couple of racehorses."

Caitlyn snorted. "If the horseshoe fits! Get it?"

Alexa pinched the bridge of her nose. "And people wonder why I don't come home more often."

"Anyway," Caitlyn's friend continued, "Russ attended their private high school. I went to the regular high school, so I had to learn about Royal's young elite through Russ. Apparently, your sister and Jackson were a power couple."

"This is illuminating," Caitlyn said. "I didn't know my big sister was one-half of a high school power couple. How did you immortalize it? Carve 'A-JACKS 4 EVER' on an oak tree?"

"We were *not* a couple of any kind," Alexa said frostily. "And we're not back at anything. This is a friendly game."

"If it's so friendly, why are you going for blood?" Jackson asked.

Alexa moved her rook straight and across, capturing Jackson's last remaining pawn. "It's my nature. Get used to it."

Jackson gave up. Instead of the board, he studied Caitlyn's know-it-all friend. She had blond hair, blue eyes and a little smirk that very much reminded him of his old buddy. "Of course. You're *Russ*'s little sister."

Her smile broadened. "You can call me Alice. And I'm not that little. If you're into chess, I'm willing to learn. Call me."

Caitlyn's eyes cut to her. "Excuse me. He's found a partner."

"Your sister doesn't live here. She's probably leaving soon."

"You don't know that," Caitlyn hissed.

Alexa clasped her hands together. "You both need to go."

"So rude!" Caitlyn cried. "I went out of my way to find you."

"You've found me and I'm fine."

"You're more than fine! You're rekindling an old flame, just as I predicted."

Jackson laughed. Drunk Caitlyn was a trip.

"Jackson isn't an old flame," Alexa asserted.

"He might be a new one!" Alice chimed.

Caitlin raised her glass. "To new beginnings!"

Alexa buried her face in her hands. Jackson couldn't remember the last time he'd had so much fun.

"A-JACKS," Caitlyn said. "It's kind of cute."

"Thanks," Jackson said. "I came up with it."

Alexa glared at him. "Are you kidding me? You came up with that, too? Didn't you have any hobbies?"

Jackson grinned at her. "When you put it that way, it does sound juvenile."

"It sounds juvenile any way you put it."

"Come on!" Caitlyn protested. "It has a good ring to it."

Alice sought his eyes. "It's no wonder you're in PR. You're a natural."

Alexa reached for a pawn. "You're in PR?"

Jackson's reaction surprised him. He would have liked her to follow his career as closely as he had followed hers.

Alice answered on his behalf. "He's the owner and CEO of Strom Management. It's a well-known public relations firm."

"I'm sure it is."

Caitlyn draped an arm over Alexa's shoulders and squeezed. "Don't get snippy."

Finally, it was the aroma of barbecue that put an end to Alexa's torture.

Caitlyn hopped to her feet. "The cook-off! Come on, Alice. We can't miss it!"

Alexa waved goodbye. "I won't miss you!"

Caitlyn blew her a kiss and promised to return. Jackson had no doubt she'd make good on her promise, but he had no intention of sticking around to find out.

He stood and extended a hand. "Come on. Let's go."

"Where are we going?"

"To the cook-off."

"Oh, no," she said. "I'm not a cook-off type of girl."

"You are when you're with me," he said. "There are ribs calling my name."

"Can't we just order some?"

"You've been away from Texas too long, lady," Jackson said. "Barbecue has to be hot off the grill."

"What about the game?"

He studied the board. "It's your move. Go ahead and finish me."

Her gaze flickered from the board to his face. "I take no pleasure in this."

"Like hell you don't."

With a swift hand, she moved her queen across the board in a diagonal line and checked his king. Jackson clapped. She may not take pleasure in this, but he most certainly did.

Three

Standing in the heat with barbecue smoke wafting in the air, eating meat off the bone and fingers sticky with sauce just wasn't Alexa's idea of fun. Somehow, she was enjoying herself. She'd rather choke on a rib than admit it, though. Jackson played a big part. Eating off his loaded plate, a frozen margarita in one hand, and laughing at his inane observations felt like the most natural thing in the world.

"My favorite so far is number two." He noted his preference on a scorecard.

Number two was an entry called Bourbon Lovers. "Don't be ridiculous. You just love bourbon."

"Exactly."

"The flavor profile isn't complex enough."

"Alexa, we're talking ribs."

"It's a competition. They ought to aim higher."

"Which is your favorite?"

"Not sure. Let's try the one with papaya sauce."

"You couldn't pay me to. Tropical fruit and meat don't mix."

"But bourbon does?"

Jackson gave a low and dirty laugh. "Bourbon mixes with everything."

Alexa laughed, too.

A country band was covering a classic rock song. The music drowned out her laughter and the party din. There were no strangers here. Every face in the crowd was familiar. Each person she'd bumped into brought back a memory, and not all were unpleasant. Her siblings were here, scattered about. Her oldest brother, Jonathan, had come around to say hello. Not one to ever take a day off from the ranch, it was nice to see him out and about. He'd bumped fists with Jackson and chatted about football before taking off. A while later, her brother Jayden's grinning face had appeared on a jumbotron. One of the day's features had been a prerecorded video series. TCC members shared their thoughts on the meaning of charity. Jayden's contribution was exceptionally uninspiring. Alexa would have strong words for him later.

From somewhere deep in the crowd, someone hollered, "Woo-hoo! A-JACKS is back at it!"

Alexa shook her head. "If we're not careful, they'll think we're a couple."

"They'll think what they want whether we're careful or not."

"True." In Royal, rumors took flight without a drop of truth to fuel them.

"Stop worrying and try this one. Number five. Tell me it's not the best you've ever had."

He held out a rib, and Alexa bit from it. She chewed without tasting, a hunger of another kind taking over her.

"It's good. Right?"

She nodded. "So good."

"No papaya. That's smoked paprika."

The full flavor exploded in her mouth. "I think this might be my favorite."

Jackson winked. To fight off the urge to kiss him, Alexa cooled down with a sip of frozen margarita and looked away.

Caitlyn waved to her from the dance floor. She and Dev were laughing and twirling. Dev was handsome: black hair, brown skin and gleaming eyes. Caitlyn was radiant, laughing uncontrollably at something Dev had whispered in her ear.

Screw them both.

The band took a break, and the jumbotron lit up for another short episode of "What Charity Means to Me." The lavish pool party was a fundraiser, after all.

"Will I have the pleasure of seeing your face on the big screen?" Alexa asked Jackson.

His eyes lingered on her face. "You have the pleasure of seeing my face up close and personal. Isn't that enough?"

Alexa had stopped breathing, but she did not flinch. A sharp negotiator, both in her personal and professional life, she didn't banter about. When she wanted something, she asked for it in a direct manner, outlining clear terms. But did she want this? She had a lot on her mind. Her career had taken an unsavory turn.

Her family was fighting off a legal challenge that could upend all their lives. Today was fun, sure. Tomorrow, she had to get back to work.

As it turned out, no face was projected on screen. Instead of yet another earnest speech on the virtues of giving back or paying it forward, they were treated to a woman's anguished confession of love.

"Jonathan is amazing. He just is... I can't explain it, but I can see myself with him. He would make a great husband and has father material written all over him."

A hush fell over the crowd, followed by whispered conversation carrying wild speculation. Alexa reached out and grabbed Jackson's arm. "Did I hear correctly?"

"You and everybody else here, I bet."

Well, they'd been treated to an episode of "What Jonathan Means to Me." The woman couldn't be talking about her brother. There had to be more than one Jonathan in all of Royal. "You don't think she meant my Jonathan, do you?"

"Oh, Alexa." He wiped at a smudge of sauce on her cheek with the pad of his thumb. "I've never seen this side of you."

Alexa swatted his hand away and looked around for Jonathan. Wherever he was, he must be the subject of tons of unwanted attention. Jayden would've *loved* this, but Jonathan was a quirky one. Divorced and, frankly, still pissed off about the divorce, he'd been single for a while now.

Jackson looked around for a waiter. The paprika had finally gotten to him. He needed a cold drink. Alexa offered him her frozen margarita and, only ever wanting to be helpful, brought her glass to his lips. Their eyes locked as he took that first sip. She noticed how deep those brown eyes were. A girl could swim in them.

Jackson slipped her mind...until Caitlyn scurried over and crashed into them both. Ice-cold margarita splashed and spilled down Jackson's shirt and the bodice of her bustier top.

"Sorry, guys!" Caitlyn grabbed a fistful of cocktail napkins from a passing waiter's tray and shoved them into their hands. "I came as fast as I could. Did you hear what that woman said?"

The poor girl was hyperventilating. Alexa urged her to take a breath and calm down. "I'm sure she wasn't talking about our Jonathan. He hasn't seen any action since the last administration."

Jackson peeled off his wet shirt. The man's chest was solid granite.

Caitlyn dismissed Alexa's comment. "It sounded like Natalie Hastings. I've *seen* her make eyes at Jonathan."

Alexa bit back a laugh. "Like...heart eyes?"

"Shut up. You know what I mean."

All Alexa knew was that Jackson was half-naked, thanks to Caitlyn. Seriously, she was grateful to her sister. So much so, her head was spinning.

The jumbotron went dark, and Aubrey Collins, the emcee, rushed onto the elevated wooden podium set up for the band. She tapped on the microphone. "This is exciting, huh?" The crowd was too busy gossiping to respond. "Quick announcement. The cook-off is nearing a close. Now is a good time to turn in your scorecards."

Jackson went away to turn in their votes. He returned with a confirmation. "The general consensus is Natalie Hastings is carrying a torch for Jonathan. *Your* Jonathan."

"Good work," Caitlyn said. "What did you think about the bourbon ribs?"

"Top of my list. Smoked paprika comes second."

"I agree. It was too spicy."

Alexa would not be distracted by barbecue sauce. "Someone tell that poor woman she's wasting her time. Jonathan is happily single."

"He's stuck in a rut," Caitlyn said. "It's not the same thing. For sure he'll hate all this attention, though."

"Is he still here?"

"I don't know. I'll check."

"I'll come with you."

"Don't even think about it!" Caitlyn snapped. "You stay here with him."

Alexa watched Caitlyn dash off, then turned to Jackson. He shrugged. "You're stuck with me."

"It feels like a lot is going on."

"Want to give the bourbon ribs another chance?"

"Are you kidding?"

"I don't kid about barbecue."

Alexa pinched the bridge of her nose. "If I agree, could we go back to the cabana to cool off?"

"We'll do whatever you like."

She signed heavily. It came out sounding imperious, even to her ears. "Fine. I'll do it."

Alexa gave the ribs a second chance. They weren't half-bad. She wiped her fingers clean. "Happy now?"

His handsome face cracked open with a smile. "I can't remember a time I've been happier."

The emcee returned to the microphone. "Ladies and gentlemen! Your attention, please! It's time to announce the results of the annual TCC rib cook-off!"

"My money's on Bourbon," Alexa said.

Jackson peeled away from her. "No way! I made you a believer?"

"Not a chance, but I know better than to bet against it."

"Okay. We'll see."

The emcee cleared her throat. "This year's winner is—"

A crack, a crash and a crazy commotion—the podium caved, swallowing Aubrey Collins whole. Alexa gasped. Next thing, Jackson was telling her to stay back. Then he tore off to assist. Alexa had no intention of staying back. She took off in search of Caitlyn. Had her sister been anywhere near the podium when it collapsed? Or was she safe with Dev? And where were Jonathan and Jayden?

She found all four back at her cabana. They'd been looking for her. There were her people: her aggravating brothers, her annoying sister and her nice-enough, about-to-be brother-in-law. Alexa rushed to them, and they all started talking at the same time, sharing what they'd witnessed and from where. Jackson returned with news that the emcee was okay. Paramedics were on-site, and Aubrey was receiving medical attention. There was nothing more to be done.

One by one, her siblings peeled away to check in on friends. Alexa reached out to Jackson. He folded her in his arms and whispered, "Are you okay?"

She smiled up at him. "I like you, Jackson Strom."

"Not what I asked, but I'll take it."

She liked how easygoing he was. She liked that he liked bourbon ribs. She liked the way he'd run toward danger, not away from it. And she liked how gracefully he'd lost at chess. So, yes, A-JACKS was back at it.

"Let me take you home," he said.

She glanced down at the chessboard. "Don't you want a rematch?"

"Never mind that," he said. "I've already won."

Four

The following morning, Alexa woke up with a sharp headache. By contrast, her memories were fluid and hazy. Had she dreamed the previous day's events? Had she really attended a wild pool party with love declared on a jumbotron and a collapsing podium that sent a poor woman plunging to her peril? What about Jackson Strom? Had she fantasized about him showing up at her cabana with a chilled bottle of Prosecco and smoldering hot smile?

She stumbled to the bathroom and splashed cold water on her face. There was no time to waste. A hot shower, coffee, toast and more coffee should take care of it. Alexa had work to do and a small window of opportunity to do it. She was not in town to frolic at the country club, flirt with men or sip cocktails at pool parties. She was tasked with a serious mission. And the sooner she was done with it, the sooner she could return to Miami and deal with the unfinished business there. With so much to deal with, stress had her cornered. At times, she had to rely on special relaxation apps just to regulate her breathing. It was no wonder she'd let loose yesterday.

Her family and the Grandins had recruited her to handle a crucial matter. In the shower, she massaged shampoo into her hair and worked through the details in her mind. It was her mental process, start from the beginning and work through, catching holes in her hypotheses and any missing links. It started with Jackson—*Damn it!* It started with Heath Thurston. Shampoo stung her eyes, and as she rinsed it out, she repeated the name. *Heath Thurston. Heath Thurston.*

She had to get it together.

Heath Thurston, a local upstart rancher, had delivered legal documents to the Grandins, asserting ownership of the oil rights to the Grandins' and the Lattimores' ranches. Sadly, this sort of checked out. The Grandins had hired an investigator, who discovered that Victor Grandin had conferred the oil rights to Heath's mother, Cynthia Thurston. To top it off, Alexa's grandfather Augustus had signed off as a witness to the transaction. It had happened a long time ago. Her grandfather and Victor Grandin were the only two men who could clear this up. But Victor was dead and her grandfather's memory was impaired due to age.

Why would they do this? Why would these smart, savvy businessmen hand over rights of inestimable value to a total stranger? Well, as it turned out, Cynthia Thurston wasn't a stranger, at least not to Victor's son, David. She'd given birth to his love child, and that made her family. However, turning over oil rights to avoid a little child support and a lot of scandal was rather extreme.

Alexa was an environmental lawyer with some experience in litigating land use, but nothing had ever been as convoluted as this. The Grandins had hired her to represent their interests. She would have done it for free. The families had been neighbors and best friends for decades. If this proved to be true—if Heath Thurston had a rightful claim to the oil beneath the properties— he would not prove to be as patient as the late Cynthia. He would act on it, and where would that leave them?

Alexa may not be involved in the family business, but she understood that ranching was grueling, back-breaking work that often came at great personal cost. The hope was that one generation would hand the lands on to the next, creating generational wealth and stability. No one in his right mind would jeopardize it so thoughtlessly. The question remained: What was her grandfather thinking?

Alexa found her brothers in the dining room, already dressed and ready for work. Jayden was at the breakfast bar, scooping scrambled eggs onto a plate. "Well, look who's here," he said. "The belle of the ball."

Alexa ignored him. The room smelled of coffee. She poured herself a generous cup. "Where's Mom?"

"Farmers market."

"For real?" She tried and failed to imagine her mother perusing the stalls in designer sandals and sunglasses, sampling local cheeses.

"I caught her on the way out," Jonathan said. "She said something about heirloom tomatoes."

Jayden approached and nudged her in the ribs. "So about last night?"

"What about it?"

"Don't hold back. Give us the details."

"I'd rather talk about Jonathan's night and the very public declaration of love made over the loudspeaker."

Jonathan groaned. Jayden folded over with laughter. "Alexa, you go straight for the jugular! I love having you home."

Jonathan stood up from the table. "Can't do this now. I've got work to do."

Alexa did not back down. "A woman declares her undying love for you. What's your next move?"

"Nothing."

"Nothing?" she and Jayden cried in unison.

"Nothing at all. Like it never even happened."

"That is some weak sauce game, if you ask me," Jayden said.

"No one's asking you," Jonathan retorted. "It's sweet she thinks I'm amazing, but it ends there."

"The woman wants you to father her children, Jonathan," Alexa said. "That's your cue to make a move."

"What's your next move with Jackson Strom?" Jonathan asked.

Just the mention of Jackson's name and she was in his arms again, feeling protected and safe. Alexa cleared her throat. "He's just an old high school friend, guys."

"Wow!" Jayden exclaimed. "That's how you're going to play it?"

Jonathan laughed. "You're at risk of committing perjury, Counselor."

"It's the truth!"

"I know what I saw," Jayden said. "You two were fire!"

Alexa called his bluff. "Give me a break. You were nowhere near us yesterday."

"True," he conceded. "But I had eyes on the ground."

"You mean Caitlyn?"

"Exactly."

Alexa topped off her coffee cup. "Caitlyn is wearing rose-colored glasses. You can't take her word for anything. Jackson and I were just catching up."

Jayden turned to Jonathan. "They used to call them A-JACKS, you know. They had a thing going."

"A-JACKS…" Jonathan raked his fingers through his morning stubble. "I kind of like it. Has a nice ring to it."

"I thought you were too busy to chat," Alexa said.

"I'm already out the door," he said. "Have a good day!"

Jonathan left the dining room. In jeans, boots and a rumpled T-shirt, he was dressed for a day's work on the ranch. It was his whole life. The thought that some outsider could wave a piece of paper laying claim on their property enraged Alexa. It wasn't fair.

"For what it's worth," Jayden said, "I approve. You and Jackson have my blessing."

As if she needed his approval. "Save your blessings for Caitlyn and Dev. I'm only in town for a few weeks this time, and I'm not looking to complicate my life with a local boy."

"I wouldn't be so cocky," Jayden said. "Us local boys have our ways."

Augustus was in his favorite rocking chair on the back patio. At ninety-four, he was always neatly dressed and expertly groomed.

His best friend, Victor Grandin, had died a few short

months ago. Heath Thurston hadn't waited to start brandishing about the deed to the oil rights. In fact, he got things going by having papers delivered the day of the man's funeral, as one does. The jerk! With Victor gone, only one living witness remained: Augustus. Although Alexa's family had a vested interest in discovering the truth, she was cautioned by her grandmother Hazel to "go easy" on her husband. Still physically strong, his memory was fading.

"Good morning, Grandpa!"

"Good morning to you, darling girl!"

Hmm… Did he know she was Alexa? "Would you like to go for a walk?"

"I'd love it."

She offered him her hand. If given a choice, he would rather sit in his chair until lunch and, after lunch, return to his chair and sit there until dinner. His doctor had recommended daily exercise. Alexa gladly took her turn to give her grandmother a break in watching over Augustus.

"Come on," she said encouragingly.

He grasped her hand and allowed himself to be lifted off the chair. She assisted him down the single step to the yard, and they strolled the stone path that wound around her mother's rose garden.

"It's a fine morning," Augustus observed.

The day was still fresh, the oppressive summer heat held at bay. Her mother's roses perfumed the air. She'd forgotten how much she loved mornings in Royal.

Her grandfather chuckled. "Do you remember when Jayden chased you down this path? You tripped and landed in the rose bushes. You cried and cried."

So he did know who she was. She smiled. "It was Easter Sunday. Jayden went to bed without dessert."

"It was peach cobbler. His favorite."

"Every dessert is his favorite."

"That's true."

"Do you remember a man named Heath Thurston?"

Her grandfather made a face. The abrupt transition had taken him off guard. Alexa was a shrewd interrogator. She wasn't exactly known for her light touch. The first day she'd questioned him, they'd met in his study. He sat in his worn leather recliner, and she settled behind his imposing wood desk. The formal setting quickly worked against her. Augustus got defensive. So now they met on the back porch. She went over the same questions every day, trying to catch a detail here or there that he'd omitted the previous day. It was a long and tedious process, but there were no other alternatives. Her grandfather would not allow just anyone to harass him like this, so it fell on her lap to do it.

"I can't say that I do."

"Are you sure the name doesn't ring a bell?"

"I'm sure."

It frustrated Alexa to no end that her grandfather remembered every detail about their domestic life, down to the dessert served on the Easter Sunday his granddaughter fell into a rose bush, and nothing about signing away millions of dollars' worth of oil rights.

"What about Cynthia Thurston?" she continued. "Surely you've heard of her?"

"I haven't. Is she a friend you met at school?"

"Hold on," she said. "Maybe a photo will help refresh your memory."

If he couldn't remember Cynthia, how could he possibly remember any obscure transactions they'd engaged in?

Alexa reached for her phone to search for a photo of the late Cynthia Thurston online. She tapped on the internet browser. The results of her last search were still there to haunt her: Strom-Management.com. She'd looked him up while in bed last night. He was quite a successful entrepreneur. She quickly closed the browser, a blush spreading across her cheeks.

"You know what? Let's just enjoy our walk."

Her grandfather eyed her with curiosity. "What has gotten into you this morning, young lady?"

"Nothing. A little tired from yesterday."

"If you're tired, it doesn't show. You're glowing."

Alexa doubted that very much. Still, she thanked her grandfather.

"You look happier than I've ever seen you."

"Do I?"

"Would I lie?"

By omission? Yes. She was sure of it.

"I attended a pool party yesterday and got a little sun. Maybe that's it."

"Whatever it is, keep at it," he said. "It's nice seeing you like this. When you graduate at the top of your class, you'll have the whole world at your feet."

They paused by the stone birdbath. Augustus took a seat on a nearby bench.

"Grandpa, I'm a lawyer with a big firm in Miami."

"Yes, of course!"

She might be losing him.

"Are they treating you okay at work?"

She joined him on the bench and took his hand. For a man with poor eyesight and memory deficits, how did he know where to find her soft spots? "I couldn't ask for better. Don't worry about me. I'm a little tired. That's all."

"You're a Lattimore. We don't tire easily."

No lies were detected there! Her grandfather had worked well into his nineties and turned over the ranch to Alexa's father only after his faltering memory proved to be a problem.

"Are you happy in your personal life?"

It warmed Alexa's heart that her grandfather was concerned about her. She had always felt like an outsider in her own home. When she left for college, her family had not worried about her, certain that she was doing well.

"Are you?" Augustus repeated.

"Absolutely happy!" she replied. "Besides, I'm here to get answers out of you, not the other way around."

"I'm sorry I haven't been more helpful, Barbara. I just don't know what all the fuss is about."

Yes, she'd lost him. He thought Alexa was her mother. "I love spending time with you," Alexa replied before kissing him on the cheek.

Her grandmother came walking down the path. "There you are, Augustus. It's time for your medication."

Alexa helped her grandfather onto his feet, and Hazel escorted him back into the house. She sank down onto the bench and watched them go. The day ahead was as wide and open as the unencumbered lands of the ranch. The private investigator on the case had not yet returned with news. Until he did, there wasn't much for her to do. Maybe she'd visit with Layla Grandin and catch up with her.

Her phone chimed with a text message alert, the number saved under JACKSON STROM_DO NOT ANSWER ON FIRST RING. Clearly she was a bit tipsy when they'd exchanged numbers at her door last night. There were no instructions as to what to do if and when he texted, so she stared at the phone and read the short message over and over, searching for hidden meanings and subtext.

You owe me a rematch.

Five

You forfeited your rematch. Besides, you owe me a meal that is not ribs.

Jackson dropped his phone onto his desk. *Okay, game on.* He'd spent last night plotting, trying to come up with ways to see Alexa again. He couldn't afford to play it cool. Who knew how long she'd be in town? Back when they were kids in school, he'd missed out on the opportunity to get to know her. Instead, he'd baited and challenged her at every turn. He didn't regret it necessarily. He'd had fun with it; plus, it had upped his game. But he wasn't a kid anymore.

He texted back. Dinner tomorrow?

Her reply came right away. Lunch today. Pick a spot and I'll meet you there.

He sent her an address, and they agreed on a time.

If she thought he couldn't make a simple friendly lunch into something special, she didn't know him very well.

Alexa had arrived at the restaurant before him and was waiting at their table. Dressed for a business meeting in a tailored cream blazer worn over a silky cream blouse, with her dark hair swept up in a bun and eyes narrowed on her phone, she was stunning but intimidating. For the length of a heartbeat, he was that insecure kid again. It took courage to take the next step.

He joined her at the table. It was one of the best, removed from the business on the main floor and close to a large window with a view of a water feature in the courtyard.

"Jackson," she said without looking up. "Have a seat. I've been looking over your résumé."

Had he been summoned to HR?

He sat across from her. "Have you?"

She glanced up. Her gaze swept over him appreciatively for a hot second. "It's all here on your website."

"I'm sitting right here and you're looking me up?"

"I would have done it behind your back, but why bother hiding it?" she said. "I'm curious about you. You're actually quite accomplished."

He took a sip from his water glass. "I like to think so."

"I see you've won quite a few awards for your work."

"What else do you see?"

She set the phone down. "I'm trying to say that I'm proud of you."

He leaned forward. "Well, just say it."

"You did good. Now don't let that go to your head."

"Oh, too late. My head is as big as all of Texas."

"You're such a Texas boy."

"And proud of it."

The waiter arrived with the lunch menu and a separate wine list. Alexa reviewed both and selected a crisp sauvignon blanc and mini crab cakes without a second's hesitation. She knew her mind. It was one of the things he loved about her. Correction: it was one of the things he *liked*. Jackson went for the wine and held off on an appetizer.

"You know," she said, "when I ruled out ribs, I wasn't requesting foie gras. We could have gone for burgers."

"You're not dressed for burgers."

She looked down at her outfit, the corners of her mouth turned down in the cutest little frown. "This is just how I dress."

"Do you ever take a day off?"

"Sure. Once a month, I treat myself to a spa day."

Jackson nodded. "That sounds about right."

"What do *you* do to relax?" she asked, suddenly defensive.

"I drive out to my cabin and unplug."

"Tell me more. How does Jackson Strom 'unplug,' exactly?"

"I swim, go for long runs, fish, grill, pour a bourbon, play records at night, sleep under the stars…"

She looked down at her tightly clasped hands. "That sounds nice, actually."

"It's like a spa getaway, but without the candles and moody music."

"Well, now you've ruined it for me. I need candles."

"Candles are hit or miss with me. I'm not into strong floral scents."

"Not all candles smell like a rose garden."

"Which are your favorites?"

"Lavender is my all-time favorite," she said. "I love a fresh lavender scent."

Jackson felt the stirrings of a new idea. "If I filled the place with lavender-scented candles, would you come with me to my cabin for a few days?"

"You wouldn't have to fill the place," she said. "One or two pillars would be enough. But my answer is no."

"Any particular reason?"

"I don't need a reason to say no."

"So this is a knee-jerk sort of rejection?"

"I'm here to work, not to wander in the woods."

The Grandins had recruited her to fight off a claim against their property's oil rights—that much he knew. It was the sort of thing that could start a war in their small corner of the world. Apparently, they were going after the oil under Alexa's family's ranch as well. He didn't blame her for taking the job seriously.

"What's the status of the case?" he asked.

"We're waiting for a PI's next report. When we know more, we'll take action."

"So you're in a holding pattern. Just waiting around."

She shifted in her seat. "That's right."

"Couldn't you wait at my cabin?" he suggested.

"No offense. I prefer to enjoy running water and a couple streaming apps while I wait."

He blinked, not understanding. Then he broke out in laughter that was louder than acceptable at the intimate French restaurant.

She pursed her full lips, trying hard to suppress a smile. "I'm just saying."

"The cabin has all the conveniences of the modern world, including Wi-Fi, satellite TV and cell service," Jackson said. "You won't miss a call or an episode of a show. And it has the most perfect firepit by the lake. You can have a glass of wine while looking at the stars."

"How far away is it?"

"About a three-hour drive. That's not so bad, right?"

She measured it out in her mind. "That's about the distance of Miami to Orlando."

"Let's forget Florida and focus on our great state. I want you to see the beauty of living in Royal."

"You're not going to sell me a time-share, are you?"

"I couldn't sell you iced lemonade in the Sahara."

"That's not really a compliment," she said. "Okay. Let's say I agree. Hypothetically, of course."

"Of course."

"Because I haven't agreed to anything."

"Understood." Jackson was ready for a fight. Alexa was so smart, yet she couldn't walk through an open door without a hypothetical swift kick in the ass.

"How long would we be gone?"

"We could leave on Friday and make a weekend of it," he said. "I like to enjoy my Sundays, so we could take the road early Monday morning."

"Monday morning? Don't you have a business to run?"

"Let me worry about that," Jackson said. "What do you think?"

"Under normal circumstances, I'd turn you down flat," she said. "You know that, right?"

"Absolutely." He was under no illusions. Still, he was curious. "What circumstances are we working under?"

"My sister is driving me crazy."

"Little Caitlyn?" He balked. "Come on! She's adorable."

"She's sugar and spice and a pain in the ass ever since she's found love with Dev."

"Are you closer to your brothers, then?"

She hesitated, considered her answer. "Not really."

Jackson couldn't believe it. "Isn't that the point of having a bunch of siblings? To have this big ready-made clan?"

"We're just so different," she said. "They would have loved roughing it at your cabin."

"Again, we won't be roughing it."

The cabin had been in his family for generations, and he stood to inherit it. Over the decades, it had been renovated several times. The property bordered a lake, and each room offered a view of the surrounding woods. The bedrooms were spacious; the kitchen, state of the art; and the backyard was fitted with a grill and a pizza oven no one ever used.

The waiter placed her appetizer before her, giving her the excuse to ignore his question. She picked up a fork and sliced a golden crab cake in two. "Want to try this?" she said. "It looks delicious."

"No, thank you. I'm allergic to shellfish."

She dropped the fork onto the plate. "You are?"

"Yes, I am," he said. "Don't let that stop you. It does look delicious."

She shook her head in wonder. "There's so much I don't know about you."

"Here's your chance to find out," he said. "Come away with me."

"So…what's in it for you?"

"Excuse me?"

"I get a peaceful retreat, but you get stuck with me. How's that a fair exchange?"

Behind the bite of her words, Jackson detected something new. She was insecure. That was not a word he would have ever associated with the great Alexandra Lattimore. He'd thought her impervious to what people thought or said about her, a true ice queen. But what did he know about human nature at sixteen? Back then, he took people at face value, never guessing at any hidden depths. He tried to reassure her. "Getting stuck with you is the best part."

The waiter returned to take their orders. While he selected a bottle of wine for their meal, she looked at him coolly from across the table. He was so aware of her. At all times, he was aware of her shifts in mood and how they played out on her face. The waiter moved to another table. She picked up her fork and twirled it. "In order for me to consider your offer—and I am considering it—I need clear terms and conditions."

"Alexa, you're not leasing a mobile phone. Can't a friend take you on a trip without drafting legal papers?"

"Apparently not."

"Okay. Shoot."

"I may have to leave at a moment's notice for work or other family obligations. If that happens, I apologize in advance. Please don't try to make me feel guilty. I'll book an Uber and be on my way."

Jackson nodded. He could work with that. "One— there's no Uber. We're going to a lake cabin, not the

Cattleman's Club. Two—I'll drive you back to town, no questions asked."

"I'll need my own room."

"That's a given. You'll have a suite to yourself."

She nodded and took a sip of water.

"Are you done?" Jackson asked. "Because I have some conditions of my own."

"Which are?"

"We stop all this talk about conditions," he said. "I propose we spend a weekend at my lake cabin to chill out and get to know each other better. That's the offer. Either you accept it or reject it wholesale. I won't have you controlling every little thing."

He searched her face for a reaction. There was none. Alexa was giving him award-winning poker face.

The waiter brought their wine, poured a bit in a glass for her to try. She did so robotically, nodding her approval. He filled both their glasses and left.

"All right," she said. "No terms. No conditions. But if there's fishing—"

"Oh, there'll be fishing."

"I won't be handling any live bait. That's my bottom line."

Jackson tore a piece of bread and popped it in his mouth. "What's your stance on midnight swims?"

"I don't have one," she said. "I'll be exhausted from all the needless fishing, so I'll be dead asleep by midnight."

Six

Jackson Strom was just as attractive in a deep blue business suit as in a T-shirt and swim shorts. That was an equation she couldn't puzzle out. It was the swagger. She'd spotted him as he made his way across the restaurant floor. The way he carried himself—head high, back straight, strides long and sure—had been enough to give her a mini-stroke. Her brain froze midthought, and nothing went right after that. She'd agreed to go away with him for a weekend at a… On the drive home, Alexa paused to check her mental notes. She'd agreed to go away with him for a weekend at his *cabin*, where they would hike, fish, grill and go for midnight swims. That couldn't be right.

Was it too late to get out of it? No. Never. She was a Lattimore. It was her prerogative to change her mind. If she didn't want to go on a fishing trip with her old

high school nemesis, no one could make her. She'd call
Jackson and tell him… Tell him what? Hmm… Her
grandfather needed her for…huh…

Her phone rang. The caller ID flashed on the dashboard monitor of her father's old Mercedes: JACKSON
CALLING_ DO NOT ANSWER ON FIRST RING.

Damn it!

She answered on the first ring. "Hello."

"Hey. I'm arranging for them to stock up the fridge
in advance of our arrival. Is there anything you need?
A specific type of coffee or milk?"

"Actually, Jackson…"

"Yes?"

"Actually…"

"Go on. I'm listening."

"I don't know what got into me back there in the
restaurant."

"The crab cakes, maybe?"

"They were delicious. Too bad you're allergic."

Why was she stuck on that small point? He had an
allergy. So what? It struck her as the tip of the iceberg
made of all the things she did not know about Jackson
Strom. She didn't know this person. The Jackson who
lived rent free in her memories was a figment of her
imagination. Unknowable. The person who had invited
her to lunch had a sense of humor, food allergies and
strong opinions on candles. The question remained:
Did she want to get to know this person better? Was it
worth her time? Yes or no?

"You can talk to me, Alexa," he said. "What's troubling you?"

She gripped the leather steering wheel. That question
had depths that she did not want to explore. Alexa pulled

into the parking lot of the nearest big-box store and cut the engine. "I'm not a lakeside cabin–type of girl," she blurted. "There! I said it. I'm not that girl and I don't think I'd be much fun, so really what I'm saying is—"

"You're chickening out."

"That's not what I'm doing." Adults didn't "chicken out." They made sound decisions taking into account their fears and anxieties. It wasn't the same thing. "It's just, I'm a city girl. I don't like anything outside the urban core. I need museums, shops, bistros, theaters, all of it."

"Alexa, take a breath," he said. "You're freaking out."

"Exactly!" she snapped. "I'm freaking out!"

"Well, don't. If anything, I'm in the vulnerable spot."

"How do you figure?"

"I'm trying to share an experience with you. What if you hate it as much as you say?"

Alexa hadn't even considered this or factored in his feelings in any way. She'd figured it was all fun and games on his part.

"I won't hate it," she admitted. "It all sounded dreamy until you roped me into it."

"Okay. That's a start."

"What if it gets all weird and awkward and tense? You and I don't have the best track record."

"We don't have to spend every waking hour antag-onizing each other," he said. "How about we set aside chunks of time to be alone?"

"That could work."

Alexa mulled it over. He could take a hike and she could listen to podcasts or read undisturbed, preferably by the firepit that he'd described earlier.

"For it to work, we only have to want it to."

He had a point. There was no reason to argue against it. She let out a dramatic huff.

"Listen," he said. "I have a confession."

"You don't know the first thing about playing chess," she offered.

"Which is why you can beat me so easily," he said. "You're no grand master."

Alexa was teary with laughter. "True!"

Jackson's laughter poured through the speakers. He was always quick to laugh at life—and at himself. It was one of the things that had endeared him to her. But the laughter stopped abruptly, and his tone turned serious. "I want to get to know you."

"Since when?" she asked.

"Since always," he replied. "I screwed up with you. I know."

"Generally, it takes two to screw."

His low laughter tumbled through the car speakers. "Alexa... I'm starting to think there's lava under all that ice."

"Don't tell anyone. I have a reputation to uphold."

He laughed and warmth spread throughout her chest. She switched on the ignition and cranked up the AC. The seats had a massage function, and she switched it on, too.

"Do you want to get to know me?" he asked.

She had been wrestling with that question for over twenty-four hours now. "Yes. I do."

"Then let's head out to the cabin," he said. "During the day, we'll do our own thing. At night, I'll light a fire, we'll sip whiskey, stay up late and talk."

"I'll have a white wine spritzer, but everything else sounds good."

"I'll add 'white wine spritzer' to the shopping list. What else?"

She completed her list, and they agreed on a time for him to pick her up on Friday. They were about to end the call when Alexa thought of one last point that needed revisiting. "How single are you really, Jackson? I don't want some angry woman showing up at the cabin, demanding to know why you're spending all this quality time with your former high school nemesis. It'll disturb my peaceful resting time."

"I'm very single. You don't have to worry about that."

"Good." A wave of relief washed over her. He was single and she was single, and they were free to get to know each other. How neat.

"And I never thought of you as my nemesis."

"Oh, really?"

"Really."

"What, then?" She was curious. The evidence hinted otherwise. Alexandra the First. A-JACKS. These were not terms of endearment.

"My better half."

He said it without a hiccup, without a moment's hesitation. Alexa was too stunned to say anything. Jackson said goodbye and promised to call her on Thursday.

Seven

On Thursday afternoon, Alexa sought out her mother. She checked the den, the kitchen and a sunroom that had been converted into a greenhouse. There, she found Caitlyn curled up on a rattan chair, sipping from a porcelain teacup.

"Hey, you," she said. "Where's Mom?"

"Yoga class."

"Mom does yoga?"

"Yep," Caitlyn said. "I know her schedule and arrange to take my afternoon breaks here while she's away. It's nice and quiet."

It was disconcerting to learn about her family's little routines. Alexa had no idea. She spoke to her mother regularly, and never once had she mentioned outings to the farmers market or yoga class. She would have never guessed that Caitlyn liked to sip tea alone, surrounded by potted plants. Alexa brushed off a bit of potting soil from a wrought-iron ottoman and sat down.

"I like your jeans," Caitlyn said.

"Thanks. It's part of a limited edition collaboration between two Italian design houses."

"I was wondering why you'd have them professionally pressed. That crease is sharp!"

Alexa didn't wear jeans. She wore tailored denim trousers. Her style philosophy was simple: she invested in quality pieces and took good care of them. "You don't expect me to toss them into the spin cycle, do you?"

"Heaven forbid," Caitlyn said. "Did you need Mom for something specific or just to talk?"

Alexa rarely sought out her mother just to talk. That might explain why she wasn't clued in. She added *talk to Mom* on her running mental to-do list.

"I need to borrow a weekender bag or carry-on case," Alexa said. "Anything light and compact."

"Going somewhere?"

This was the conversation she'd been dreading all week. She couldn't postpone it any longer.

"I'm going away with Jackson for the weekend."

Caitlyn dropped her porcelain teacup in its saucer with a clang. "Do you mind repeating that?"

"I think you heard me."

"Oh my God! A weekend getaway?" Her sister was screeching now. "How romantic!"

"Caitlyn, settle down. He invited me to his cabin to unwind."

"Unwind? Is that what the kids are calling it?"

"You're a kid. You tell me."

"Hold on one sec." Caitlyn reached for her phone. Her thumbs were flying over the keyboard.

"Who are you texting?"

"Jayden, obviously."

"Please don't."

The swoosh sound of the sent text message sealed her fate.

"This is a huge development, and we have to discuss, analyze, strategize."

Caitlyn's phone rang midsentence. She answered and Jayden's voice rushed through the phone's speaker. "Are you okay? What's the emergency?"

"I hope you're sitting down," she said, breathless. "Alexa and Jackson are going camping for the weekend."

This was how false information got disseminated. She corrected her sister. "We're going to his lake cabin. I hear it's very comfortable and spacious."

"I bet it is!" Jayden quipped.

Jayden and Caitlyn burst out laughing. Alexa smoothed back her hair and willed herself to stay calm. She had expected to get roasted, but this was next-level madness.

"Sit tight," Jayden said between bouts of laughter. "I'll be right in."

Alexa bristled. "Don't you have anything more important to do?"

"Not really!"

Caitlyn ended the call and tossed her phone aside. "You can't blame us," she said. "This is big news."

"I have no trouble blaming you."

"Come on! You two went from flirty banter at the TCC to a weekend getaway in all of five minutes. We need to know the details."

"There's not much to tell. We had lunch the other day and—"

"Stop!" Caitlyn held up a hand. "Wait for the guys."

Alexa shrugged. "Whatever."

Jayden couldn't really ditch work just to torment her, and she was confident Jonathan was above these foolish games.

Right then, the door to the sunroom flung open and her older, wiser, serious and steadfast brother Jonathan charged in. He was wearing his usual work shirt, jeans, boots and a Stetson to shield him from the sun. "Jayden called. I came as fast as I could." He grabbed a chair in a corner and dragged it over to where she and Caitlyn sat. "Tell me everything."

That night, when Jackson called to confirm their plans, Alexa asked if they could set out a bit earlier. Her siblings had been dragging her all afternoon, texting her memes, and her mother had cross-examined her when she returned from yoga. Alexa wanted to slip out early before the household awakened, ready to do their worst. He agreed. "We'll leave at six."

"I'll be ready."

"Alexa, one more thing."

"What is it?"

"I can't wait," he said. "I can't wait to be alone with you."

Alexa replayed those words in her mind until she fell asleep. When she awoke hours later to the bedside alarm, it was the first thing that ran through her mind. *I can't wait to be alone with you.*

At six, Alexa was ready and waiting. She stood out on the porch, her back against one of the two Greek-style pillars that served no purpose but to prop up her father's tremendous pride. She gripped the handle of her mother's small suitcase. Five minutes later, Jackson pulled up to the gate. She disarmed the security system with her phone app and let him through. Her heart pounded as the black SUV sped up the drive. It was a lavender morning. The sky was still dusted with stars. Jackson stepped out. In a white T-shirt and faded blue jeans, he was as fresh as dawn.

"Mornin'," he said, as jovial at 6:00 a.m. as he was at noon. He loaded her bag into the trunk and held open the passenger door for her. "Let's get out of here."

Alexa hesitated. Within the blink of an eye, she'd slipped back in time. She was seventeen and Jackson was her prom date, holding open the door to a tacky rental limo. There he was, the object of her every teenage dream. She went over and touched him, just to make sure he was real.

"Are you okay?" he asked.

"No," she said. "I was thinking... If things were different back in high school—"

"Different how?"

"If I were nicer."

"Nicer?"

"Or just plain nice," she said. "Do you think you might have asked me to prom or homecoming or whatever?"

Jackson went still, but something moved in his eyes. Alexa panicked. What was she doing stirring things up at dawn?

"Forget it!" She backed away from him. "I don't know why I said that. It's early and I haven't had coffee. Do you mind stopping for coffee along the way?"

He reached out and caught her by the waist. He pulled her close. The air between them was charged. "I didn't want *nice*. I wanted Alexandra Lattimore, the one girl who was anything but nice and who ran circles around me."

"Why didn't you say anything?"

"I was scared."

"You thought I'd reject you?"

"If I had asked you to prom or whatever, would you have said yes?"

"I don't know," she admitted. "Maybe not... Or I could have changed my mind. Only it would have been too late. You would have found yourself a less-complicated date."

"And end up having a forgettable night?"

"You would have had fun," she said. "I would have ended up hating myself."

Alexa wanted to be that person that he'd imagined, imperious and unimpressed by her peers or her surroundings, but she wasn't. She never had been. She'd lived her whole life in a self-protective mode, rejecting others before they could reject or dismiss her. She now saw it for what it was: a coward's device.

His hand fell from her waist. He stepped back and held open the car door even wider. "Aren't you happy we're not those stupid kids anymore?"

Alexa leaned forward and kissed him lightly on the lips. "You have no idea," she whispered, and slid into the waiting seat.

Eight

The cabin was Jackson's family vacation spot but also his private sanctuary—a hideout when life gave him hell. It was the one place he could go to and heal after disappointments and failures. He'd invited Alexa because he thought she might need some healing, too. Jackson couldn't put a finger on it, but he knew something was troubling her. She was stressed out. He'd seen her under pressure, and this was different. True, a pop quiz was not similar to having to protect and defend your family's estate holdings. Maybe she was afraid of letting them down. The consequences could be devastating. It was a lot to drop on her shoulders, as capable as they were. He had planned on asking her about it on the long drive through the quiet, tree-lined roads leading to the lakeside cabin. Then she'd kissed him, brushed her full lips against his, and his mind had gone blank. He could think of nothing else.

The drive had gone smoothly. Alexa sat angled toward him, hands curled around a jumbo cup of coffee, looking soft and relaxed. She was willing to talk about anything and everything except herself. For long stretches, she stared out the window, soaking in the ever-changing scenery. "So beautiful," she'd let out in a breath.

Jackson pulled over to the side of the road.

"Is something wrong? Why are we stopping? Are we there yet?"

"Almost. I want to show you something first. Let's go for a walk."

She fit the coffee cup into a holder and released her seat belt. "Let's do it."

They stepped out of the car. The heat made the air feel solid. Alexa stripped off her zippered jacket, balled it and tossed it into the back seat. She wore a fitted cream-colored tank underneath. Her shoulders were bare. Jackson reached out his hand. When she took it, he couldn't believe his luck.

They walked down a path leading to the old dock. It was obscured by overgrown weeds and wildflowers, but he knew the way. It was a popular hangout spot for local kids. His memories of summer holidays and winter breaks—days filled with swimming, fishing and long naps in the sun—all looped around this spot. The weathered dock had been restored. It wasn't as rickety as in his memory. Alexa followed him down to the edge. She offered her face up to the sun like a sunflower.

So beautiful...

"What do I have to say to convince you to go for a dip?"

She turned to him, brows furrowed. He didn't know

whether she was repulsed or intrigued. When she un-
zipped her denim shorts and wiggled them down her
long, toned legs, he had his answer.

"Try and stop me!" she cried.

Just like that, she was off. She leaped into the water,
arms stretched to the sky and ponytail flapping behind
her. Jackson was transfixed. *So damn beautiful!* Then
he snapped out of it, ripped off his T-shirt, kicked off
his sneakers and, heart pounding, dove in.

With a kitchen stocked with the best of everything,
they'd opted for grilled cheese sandwiches for dinner.
When Jackson pointed this out, Alexa balked. "This is
fine dining! We're using two types of cheddar and sour-
dough bread. I'd serve this on my best china."

"Good point," he said. "This grilled cheese ain't for
kids."

She was tossing a salad that had come pre-tossed in
a container. Her expression clouded suddenly. Was it
something he'd said?

I wonder if she wants kids. Her focus was squarely
on the baby spinach leaves, even though his mind was
on babies. *I should ask.*

The objective of this trip was to get to know each
other. There was no need to be coy about it. Naturally,
she beat him to the punch.

"May I ask you something?" she said.

"Ask me whatever you want." He slid a bottle of
white wine out of the special cooler. He didn't know
what paired well with grilled cheese. However, he knew
she liked her wines on the crisp, fruity side, and he had
stocked up accordingly. "It doesn't have to be awkward."

She lowered the salad prongs to the countertop. "I don't want to pry."

Her lips were slightly parted. When could he kiss her again? Was that a question he could ask? The kiss they'd shared earlier while swimming in the lake had left his body humming. Instead, he joined her at the kitchen island and saddled onto the bar stool next to hers. "Pry. Do your worst."

"All right," she said. "How about this. Let's make a game of it. Rapid-fire questions. You can skip one or two but no more than that."

"A game?" Jackson pensively rubbed the stubble on his chin. "You realize most people would think it strange that we need a game to communicate openly."

She shrugged one shoulder. "I don't care about most people."

They were birds of a feather. "Neither do I."

Alexa grinned. "Let's do this."

"Hold on," Jackson said, excitement working through him. "Let's make it a drinking game. Anyone who skips a question has to take a sip."

Her fast smile faltered. "Not sure about that. This could go off the rails pretty quick."

"Let's hope so."

"We need rules."

He got up to fill their wineglasses. "That's just what the world needs—more rules."

"I'm serious," she said. "We have to make sure that the information gathered here today is not misused when we're back in the real world."

"There's no chance of that." He set a glass before her. "We have a long-standing 'What Happens in the Cabin Stays in the Cabin' rule."

She rolled her eyes. "That's not specific enough. Get me a pen and paper, please."

"Alexa, really?" Jackson said, incredulous. Then he remembered who he was dealing with, and his incredulity fell away. Of course she wanted to codify this in writing. She'd probably want to call up a notary public, too.

"Pen and paper," she repeated.

"Yes, ma'am." He rummaged through a drawer and found a pad designed for grocery shopping lists with illustrated vegetables and milk cartons in the margins. He found a ballpoint pen with a missing cap in a terracotta pot on the counter. "Here you are."

Alexa got busy writing. When she was done, she reviewed her work, ripped the page from the pad and handed it to him. "Here *you* are."

"Wow…" Jackson's voice trailed off as he read what could very well be a legally binding document.

"Just sign on the line, initial each clause and don't forget to date."

Jackson read aloud. "This nondisclosure agreement (the 'Agreement') is entered into by and between Alexandra B. Lattimore and Jackson T. Strom for the purpose of preventing the unauthorized disclosure of confidential information. The parties shall hold and maintain confidential information in strict confidence. This Agreement may not be amended except in a writing signed by both parties." Jackson slapped the page down on the counter. "Lady, you are out of your mind."

"What? It's boilerplate."

"Are you going to confess to murder? Is that it?"

"No!" she protested, laughing.

"Are you living some double life in Miami?" he

asked. "Do you have a whole other family stashed away there?"

"Nothing that exciting. I promise."

"Then what is it?"

"I'm not answering any questions. You're going to have to sign on the dotted line to find out."

His heart melted at her assertive tone. Jackson signed and dated the document and handed her the pen. Alexa signed and tossed the pen aside. She then proceeded with the game. "First topic—relationships."

That was easy enough. "Hit me. I've got nothing to hide."

"Who is your first love?"

Jackson's cool demeanor cracked. He had an answer, but he couldn't bring himself to say it. Paula Colby was a college student he'd met at a party his freshman year at UT. They'd dated for three semesters before she transferred out of state. Women moving out of Texas, and out of his life, was a recurring pattern. That wasn't what had him by the throat. For all his affection for Paula, she was not his first love. "Skip."

"You've got to be kidding!" Alexa cried. "Right out of the gate? I threw you a softball!"

"Mixing your sports metaphors," Jackson observed. "You've lost your edge."

"Do you…still love her?" she asked. "Is that it?"

He had no answer for that. "I'll skip that one, too."

"Fine!" she said. "I guess you better drink up."

Jackson raised his wineglass and winked. "Cheers."

He was good at hiding his true feelings behind a smoke screen of charm.

"Guess it's my turn," she said.

"Same question," Jackson said. "Who is your first love?"

"Gregory Milford. Some friends set us up. We texted each other for months leading up to our first date—dinner and a show. It was a very New York courtship."

"What else did you do?" he said dryly. "Stroll through Central Park? Kiss in the back of cabs?"

"Kissing in the back of cabs is a rite of passage in Manhattan," Alexa said. "Anyway, we can't all have grand and mysterious love affairs with mystery women."

"Did Greg break your heart?"

Alexa avoided his eyes. She picked up her fork and stabbed at her salad. Jackson had his answer. "He broke your heart."

"Nope," she said, and bit into a slice of cucumber. "I broke his."

Jackson clapped. "Hey now!"

"It wasn't like that. We got on very well, and then things changed."

"Changed how?" he asked. Jackson wanted to know everything about this specimen of a man who had gotten Alexandra Lattimore to fall in love with him, even if it hadn't worked out.

"I don't know…" Her voice trailed off. "He wanted more than I could give. Time, energy… I was still in school, and it got to be too much. Maybe I really am made of ice."

"Don't say that. It's not true."

"Eighty-seven high school seniors can't be wrong."

"Oh, yes, they can."

"Back to you," she said. "Did your mystery woman break your heart?"

"No." He plucked a cherry tomato from the salad and popped it in his mouth.

"Is that all you're going to say?"

"Yep."

"Why are you so tight-lipped?" she demanded. "Is she rich and famous? Are you protecting her identity? Maybe she got you to sign a real NDA?"

Jackson tapped the notepad sheet. "Wait a minute. This isn't real?"

"For us it's as real as real gets."

"Okay." He made a show of relaxing his shoulders. "I'll say this—I didn't break her heart and she didn't break mine. We went our separate ways, but I've never stopped thinking about her."

His words landed on padded silence. Alexa scooped her sandwich off the plate, the melted cheese stretching thin as she pulled the halves apart. By the way she avoided his eyes, he just knew the gears of her beautiful mind were churning.

"Jackson."

"Yes?"

"Is there something you're not telling me?"

"You're the genius. You figure it out."

She dropped the sandwich onto the plate and pushed it away. "If I were a genius, I'd have life figured out."

"You don't?"

She shook her head. "Do you?"

"I try not to overthink it."

She pressed her lips together, nodding slowly. After their impromptu swim, she'd slipped on a loose-fitting white T-shirt that looked expensive and soft to the touch. She had gathered her damp hair in a braid down her back. Her face was scrubbed clean. He longed to run a fingertip along her jawline, down her neck to the dip of her collarbone. "In the spirit of not overthinking things," she said, "I've thought about you, too."

Jackson dropped his fork with a clang and reached for her. Their kiss in the lake had been scorching hot. This one was sweet and syrupy. Her tongue swept against his, turning his blood thick. He cupped the nape of her neck and tried to draw her to him, but she broke away, leaving him panting.

She pressed her palms to his chest. "I broke up with every man I ever dated."

Okay, that was worth the interruption. "How many men are we talking about?"

She did not reply. Instead, she reached for her wineglass and took a healthy sip.

Jackson pressed a fist to his mouth to keep from bursting in laughter. "We should have made this a kissing game. Think how much more fun that would have been."

She set down her glass. "There's always tomorrow."

"All right." Jackson leaned back and folded his arms across his chest. "I have a follow-up question for you."

"Go on."

"Any clue why?"

She shrugged. "No idea."

"I reckon you were scared."

"You *reckon*? Really?"

Jackson raised his hands. "You can take the boy out of Texas—"

"No, you can't," she interrupted. "You'll never leave Royal."

"Why should I? I'm happy here," Jackson replied. "Are you happy?"

She held his gaze a long while. He'd touched at something; he knew it. She reached for her glass and took a long sip.

Jackson looked away. "Next topic?"

"Sure," she said. "Do you want a family?"

"Not right away." Jackson was clear about that.

"Same," she said. "Do you have a time line in mind?"

"Somewhere in my thirties," he said. "You?"

She let out a sigh that betrayed her frustration. "No clue. It's not something I can leave to chance, but I don't even want to think about it."

"Then don't."

"It's not that easy," she said. "My family already thinks I'm a lost cause."

It was the tradition in Jackson's family, and likely hers, to marry early and have kids while still young. His mother had started to increase the pressure, moving from subtle hints to straight-up demands. It didn't help that his younger brother was engaged and expected to set a date for the next year. Jackson didn't care. He had a very clear vision of his future. He had a list of goals and experiences he wanted to have before settling down.

"Same," he said. "Screw 'em."

She offered him a conspiratorial smile that went straight to his head. "Agreed. Screw 'em."

After dinner, Jackson gave her a tour of the property. The grounds extended to the lake. His dad's boat was tethered to the dock. They competed at tossing pebbles. He won handily. She tossed her hands up in defeat. "Fine! You win!" she cried, as she jumped into the lake. He watched Alexa floating on her back, her face to the setting sun.

He quickly joined her. They splashed around for a while until he noticed that she was trembling cold. The lake was warm enough, but she was used to heated pools. "Come. I'll keep you warm." She glided toward him and snaked her arms around his neck. Fire sparked within him at the feel of her wet body. She kissed the corner of his mouth. Jackson knew the world hadn't gone silent. A small aircraft buzzed overhead, the water lapped against the dock, a dog barked madly in the distance. Still, he heard none of it. He lowered his head and kissed her full on the mouth. She parted her lips, drawing him in. He tasted her for the first time, savored her. Her kiss was languid and unhurried, but he could not prolong it without taking this too far.

Jackson released her.

Alexa startled. "Oh, God," she uttered between sharp intakes of breath. She smoothed back her hair with shaky hands and pushed out a laugh. "That got heated fast!"

That was an understatement. He dipped below surface to cool off. There was no way he could climb out of this lake otherwise. When he resurfaced, she reached for him before he could slip away again. Their fingers interlaced with ease.

"Just wanted you to know that I'm open to the possibility," she said. "Just not...right away."

"I'm open to anything," he said, and he meant it. He was open to a platonic friendship, a hookup, a full-on love affair—it was her choice. He would not pressure her for more than she could give. That was the promise he'd made to himself on the drive over to her house early this morning. He wanted her, but he was willing to seal that door shut if she didn't feel the same. Meanwhile, she had been doing the opposite work, leaving herself open to possibilities.

All those possibilities were swimming in his head now.

"I need a shower."

This was his cue. It had been a long day. It was time to give her the space she'd asked for. She went upstairs, and he remained out on the deck to light a fire in the pit. Hunched low to study the flames, he saw the last of the sunlight twinkling on the lake's sterling surface.

Jackson heard Alexa's bare feet on the wood stairs leading to the deck. He rose and turned to find her standing at the doorway, wearing nothing but a towel. Her hair was in a knot on top of her head. She looked upset. What could have gone wrong already? Had the hot water stopped working midshower?

"Everything okay?" he asked.

"There are candles in the bathroom." It was not a statement, rather an accusation. "And on my bedside table."

He didn't deny it. "Is that unusual?"

"Lavender-scented candles."

"Okay."

"My favorite."

"So you've said."

"You got them for me."

Well…he'd arranged for *someone* to get them. "I wanted you to feel welcome."

She tightened her grip on the knot of her towel. "Thank you."

"You're welcome."

"No," she said, raising her free hand to better make

her point. "I'm serious. Thank you for arranging this getaway and taking the time to make it special."

"You're welcome, Alexa."

Her gaze skidded away from him. "You've lit a fire."

He glanced over his shoulder at the leaping flames. "I'll put it out if it makes you uncomfortable."

"No, I like it."

"So do I."

Jackson was still rattled by her reaction to the candles. Such a small gesture had provoked an outsize emotional response. She could have waited until morning to say thanks. Instead, she'd stormed down the stairs, demanding answers. Was she so unaccustomed to being pampered without the hefty price of a premium spa?

"Will you be roasting marshmallows?"

"If you like," he said. "We'll make s'mores."

"I'd like that." She took a few steps backward. "I'll just go and finish up…"

"And I'll set up."

"Don't start without me!" She dashed back into the house.

Nine

Alexa hated s'mores. She hated anything sticky and sweet that could potentially stain her expensive clothes. She loved the idea of spending an evening with Jackson by a crackling fire with a glass of wine. If she had to fake love for charred marshmallows, so be it.

Oh, God! Who was she? What had she become? From dawn to dusk, she had not been herself. Tomorrow she'd regret every stupid move she'd made, from reminiscing about prom to declaring herself open to future possibilities. And why had she unraveled at the first whiff of a lavender-scented candle? Over the years, she'd offered and received candles on all sorts of occasions. It wasn't that big of a deal. It just meant that he was thoughtful, likely one of the most thoughtful people she'd ever met. Was that any reason to go charging through the house, barefoot and wrapped in a bath towel, to express her gratitude?

She dropped the towel onto the bathroom floor and turned on the shower. It was a warm, sticky night. She would likely need another shower to cool off following their fireside chat. Actually, she needed to cool off, period. Alexa promised herself the night would end with her back in her room, tucked in bed and browsing social media, as per usual. The night was *not* going to end with her tumbling into bed with Jackson.

Refreshed after showering, she was debating whether to wear shorts or a summer dress when her phone rang. It was Layla Grandin. She was calling with an update from the private investigator, Jonas Shaw. In brief, there was nothing to report.

"Sorry this is dragging," she said. "I thought there would be more for you to do."

It was Layla who'd first said they needed her to take on the case, narrowly beating out her family. For that reason, she likely felt personally responsible for Alexa's comfort and well-being. In truth, Alexa would have returned regardless. She had her own reasons, not least of which was that her family's oil rights were also in peril. Her father wasn't pleased with the current lawyer. He was an outsider who wasn't invested in the case. But for her entire life, Alexa had been her clan's outsider. Now here she was, the center of attention. It was strange.

"I'm fine," Alexa reassured Layla. "Jackson took me out to his cabin. If anything should—"

"Whoa!" Layla cried. "Mind backing up and repeating those last few words?"

Shit! She should be more discreet. Judging by her siblings' reaction, her relationship with Jackson was scorching-hot gossip. They hadn't discussed how they would handle this. Given that he was in PR, she'd let him take the lead.

"Do you remember Jackson Strom from high school?" Alexa asked.

"What do you mean, 'Do I remember Jackson Strom from high school?' I remember Jackson from just two weeks ago. We get our cars serviced at the same dealership. We grab coffee and chat while we wait. I've been trying to get him to try a chai latte. My point is, I don't need a trip down Memory Lane to remember Jackson Strom. And why is this the first I'm hearing about this? I'm one of your closest friends."

What Layla was describing was so damn pleasant. How lovely to have a standing appointment with your old high school friend, to go through the trouble of arranging appointments at the dealership just to grab a coffee and catch up. It was the sort of thing that might only happen in Royal. She cleared her throat before speaking. "My point is, we're just hanging out. It's no big deal."

"Have you gotten a good look at him?"

"Yes."

"Like, really?"

"Yes!"

"I say this with respect—he's hot."

Alexa sank down to the edge of her bed and covered her eyes with the palm of her hand. "I *know*."

She relived that moment on the old dock. She'd caught sight of him just before he dove in after her. He was breathtakingly beautiful, with the sun pouring gold on his brown skin.

"Honestly, I can't believe he's still single."

Honestly, neither could Alexa.

"You can hang out with just about anyone," Layla said. "But I'd keep my eye on Jackson. I always thought you two would make a cute couple."

"I don't know." Alexa didn't like making moves if she couldn't see straight through to the end game. It was the quality that made her a natural at chess. What chance did they have at a future? Her life was waiting elsewhere.

"I bet big money he'd ask you out to senior prom and lost big. You owe me five bucks and a chocolate bar."

Alexa was heartened her lifelong neighbor hadn't bet against her. "Who was taking bets?"

"Never mind that. It was a long time ago."

"Honestly, I keep going back and forth with this. There's no way to keep it casual. Why bother starting something if I can't see it through? I'm leaving soon enough."

She didn't want to add Jackson to the long list of men with whom she'd used her career as an excuse to brush aside.

"Your heart will know what to do."

Her *heart* would know what to do? "Oh, God," Alexa moaned. "I forgot. You're one of those people."

"What people?"

"People in love. You're like Caitlyn."

"You make it sound as if I've been infected with a zombie virus."

"I couldn't have put it better."

"Well, Josh and I are very happy. Thank you very much. I want my friends to be happy, too. Or maybe it's the stress of the case that's getting to me. I need a distraction."

Alexa wished she could reassure Layla that everything would work out in the end. However, in her experience, when so much money was involved, the moral arc of the universe bent toward greed. Heath Thurston was hunting for oil. He would stop at nothing. Alexa was not an optimist, but she wasn't a quitter. She'd made her professional reputation by being methodical and thorough. If there were loopholes to be found, even a single one, she would find it and leap through it.

Layla wished her a goodnight. "Say hi to Jackson for me!"

"I will. And I'd like to try that chai latte."

"Absolutely! We'll meet up soon."

Alexa set the phone on its charger. She decided on a dusty-rose halter dress and, after a short debate, left her room barefoot. For some reason, the rest of the house had plunged into darkness. She called out Jackson's name as she tentatively made her way down the hall and stairs. Hearing no response, Alexa stopped to assess her situation. She was a single woman, alone with a man in a dark cabin deep in the woods: the premise of every slasher film.

Suddenly…a flash of light! Alexa squeezed her eyes shut and screamed.

Jackson called out her name. A moment later, he was charging up the stairs. "Alexa! What's wrong?"

"I don't know! The house was dark and…"

"I'm setting up. Did I scare you?"

"Hell yes, you scared me!"

He took her in his arms. "Sorry, babe. God, you're shaking."

He was shaking, too, but with laughter. He had the nerve to find this funny. "Why is it dark in here? What are you setting up for?"

Jackson released her and presented her with what looked like a pink carnation snapped from its stem and secured to a bit of ribbon with a safety pin.

"What's that?" she asked.

"A corsage."

He fastened the flower to her wrist with the ribbon. Then he took her hand in his. "Alexandra Lattimore, will you be my date for prom?"

Alexa looked past Jackson's broad shoulders. There was a disco ball hanging from the ceiling over the coffee table and sending shards of silver light onto every wall. A punch bowl was set up on the kitchen island. Finally, she looked up at him. His eyes had the luster of honey. She burst into tears.

"Oh, babe…" Jackson held her close, stroking her back until she calmed down. She might have been vacillating with this a while ago, but that was done. She was swinging forward. There was no going back.

Alexa straightened up and offered him her hand. "Take me to prom."

Ten

The idea had come to Jackson in a flash. They could talk by the fire any old time, but tonight was prom night. He snipped a flower from the back garden and fastened it to a bit of ribbon. He dug out the old disco ball, a holiday staple, from a storage bin. Then he had dimmed the lights, lit a few candles and quickly downloaded a few power ballads from their high school years. That was when she'd come down the stairs and screamed. He'd nearly had a heart attack.

For the second time in a day, he was holding her quivering body close. She smelled fresh from the shower, and her deep brown skin was dewy soft. And then he'd gone and made her cry.

How had it all gone so wrong? He could've waited until their second night before scaring her to death. Jackson was about to call the whole thing off when her breathing steadied. She straightened up and swiped at the tears rolling down her cheeks. Alexa was Alexa again. Head high, she offered him her hand.

Jackson hit Play on his phone, and a power ballad that had dominated the airways their senior year rumbled through the sound system.

He turned to her. "May I have this dance?"

She arched a brow. "Were you really that smooth?"

"My dad gave me a handful of phrases," Jackson explained. "It was that or 'What's your sign?'"

She grinned, a glint of mischief in her eyes. "I'm an Aries, and my boyfriend is parking the car. He'll be back in five."

"That's all I need."

They came together, laughing. They swayed to the sound of the electric guitar. She looked up at him, her eyes bright. "You made punch?"

"It's just spiked lemonade."

The singer crooned, *"Baby, you make me crazy."*

"I bet this song had plenty of girls in tears by the end of the night."

Jackson felt uneasy. He hoped to God that tonight was the first and only time he'd made her cry. "Alexa, I've been meaning to ask…"

"What is it?"

She kept her head on his chest, and they swayed together. He stroked her back. "Did I break your heart?"

She stiffened in his arms. "You mean, back in high school?"

He nodded, his jaw rubbing her hair. Of course. When else?

She jerked away, red-faced. Jackson hoped to God

she wouldn't cry again. That was before she laughed in his face. "Get over yourself! It wasn't like that."

Relief shot through him. His crush had kept him humming all those years. Even so, their relationship had been rooted in mutual contempt. It wasn't ideal, but it balanced them out. Neither one of them had seemed eager to mess with the equilibrium.

Jackson cupped her face. "Hey, beautiful, you can stop laughing now."

Her laughter died. She drifted back into his arms. "You may not have broken my heart, but you had me wondering what if."

He brushed his nose against hers. "Same."

The ballad gave way to a pop song that was only slightly more upbeat. Alexa closed her eyes and dropped her head back. "I remember this one."

Jackson closed his eyes, too. He loved the way they moved together. He loved the feel of her in his arms. He loved her fresh scent. He loved the way she was looking at him now.

The next song on the playlist was a raging dance hit. Alexa cupped a hand over his ear and spoke over the music. "In the spirit of prom, we should grab a couple of beers and go make out in your car."

Jackson liked her thinking, but he had other plans. "In a minute. I've got a lock on prom king."

"Fool! Kiss me."

His hands moved from her waist to the sides of her face. He swept the pad of a thumb along her lower lip and waited. The air between them was charged. His heartbeat drove faster than the music. He teased her with a shallow kiss. She whimpered and he kissed her deeply. It went to his head like whiskey, but her words bobbed to the surface of his mind: *I'm open to the possibility. Just not right away.* She didn't want to rush things. Neither did he, Jackson realized.

It took everything he had to break the kiss. "Let's get you that beer."

She brought a shaky hand to her swollen lips. "Okay."

Half a beer later, Alexa was dancing on the couch.

Eleven

Fishing while managing a hangover was cruel and unusual punishment. Jackson had knocked on her bedroom door at dawn. He'd ignored her pleas for leniency and sentenced her to four hours of outdoor activities. Stretched out on his boat, legs crossed at the ankles, sunglasses on to block the harmful sun, Alexa's line dipped listlessly into the glassy lake. "This is unethical," she moaned.

"Write about it in the *New England Journal of Who Gives a Damn.*"

"Hey!" she fired back. "That's a venerable publication. Show some respect!"

He laughed. "It's not so bad, is it?"

"Whoa!" There was a sharp tug on her line. She gripped the handle of her rod.

Jackson made a face. "That bad?"

"I got a bite!" Alexa scrambled to her feet and widened her stance for better control.

Jackson was immediately at her side. "I'll help!"

"Back off. I got this."

He dropped his hands on his hips. "Let's see what you got, then."

"Just watch."

Alexa widened her stance and reeled in a largemouth bass with minimal effort. Its slick silver body flopped restlessly. Satisfied, she handed the rod to Jackson. He could take over now. She'd done her part.

Jackson was dumbstruck. "I thought you didn't fish."

Alexa shrugged and settled down on the floor of the boat. She joined her hands behind her head. "I know *how* to fish. I just don't see the point in it. There are easier ways to enjoy seafood."

"True," he said. "But no one will hand you a trophy at the end of the day."

"That little guppy is not going to earn us any trophies."

Her catch was larger than a sardine, but not by much.

Jackson studied it and turned to her. "Should we release it? Give it a fighting chance?"

"Please."

Jackson unhooked the fish and tossed it back into the water. He set down his rod and crossed the length of the boat to where she was lounging. There was no other word for it. She was lounging on a rowboat in the gentle hours of the morning. If her head weren't pounding, it would be delightful. Jackson crawled over her and rested his head on her chest. "Tell me how bad it is."

This was the one tangible benefit of their wild night partying to club music from the early 2000s under a

'70s-era disco ball: they were no longer shy around each other. Jackson touched her every chance he got. Now he was resting on her, his weight pressing into her, his words vibrating through her, and suddenly everything was so, so good.

She raked her fingers through his thick, wavy hair. "Let's just stay like this, and everything will be all right."

"Now you're getting it." He tugged at the hem of her T-shirt. "May I?"

"May you what?"

"Touch you."

He slipped a hand underneath it, the rough palm grating against her skin. Alexa shivered. He laughed quietly. "Is that a yes?"

"That's a yes, *please*."

"Such good manners."

She shifted to face him. They were so close, the tips of their noses brushed. "I've been thinking," she said.

"Go on."

"When are we going to…" Her voice trailed off. "You know."

"Sorry. I don't."

She cringed for having to say it. "Get busy."

"Ah." He raised his eyebrows. "You mean, 'go all the way?'"

"I mean sex, Jackson," she said plainly. Exasperation crept into her voice. "When are we going to have sex?"

Jackson winked. "There you go."

"Hey," Alexa said. "I know men are intimidated by strong, accomplished women, but I wouldn't have counted you among them."

"Thanks for the vote of confidence, babe."

"Are we doing this or not?"

"What's the hurry?"

"I know I said I wanted to wait, but I've changed my mind. We have a limited amount of time. We shouldn't waste it."

"We just got here yesterday."

She traced an index finger along his jawline, enjoying the feel of scruff. "If you're trying to be a gentleman, don't bother."

He brushed the tip of his nose against hers. "I'm not going to let you do it."

"Do what?" she said, as innocently as possible.

He kissed the corner of her mouth. "Micromanage this."

Alexa held his face between her hands, keeping him close. "That's not what I'm doing."

"Isn't it?"

The boat rocked, tilting to one side. She reached out and grabbed hold of him before he rolled away. His body pressed against hers opened a well of longing. For as long as she could remember, she'd longed for Jackson. It hadn't consumed her. It was a soft drumbeat barely audible under life's blaring horns. Deep inside, Alexa knew very well that she'd marched to that beat, allowed it to dictate her steps. No man had ever been brilliant, witty or charming enough to hold her attention for long. She had never outright compared the men in her life to the boy she'd crushed on through school, but now that she'd held him close, felt his body, tasted his kiss, all the pieces fit in place.

"I want to seize the day," she said. "Opportunities like this don't come around too often, Jackson."

"Alexa, you're not calling the plays on this."

"Why not? I'm so good at it."

"You want to cross me off your list, and I have other plans for us."

"What plans?"

"I want to take my time and see where this goes."

This goes nowhere! Alexa had come close to shouting the words. Nothing more could come of this. He lived in Royal, and she did not. Why should that stop them from enjoying the present?

Jackson pushed back onto his heels, sat in place and picked up the oars. He started to row them to shore with rhythmic smooth strokes.

Alexa propped herself up on her elbows. *For as long as you want it...* She was beginning to understand. He thought she was toying with him or that maybe she just wanted to hit it and quit it. Even after last night, he still thought that way.

When they made it back to the house, she followed him up the beach and along the granular path leading straight up to the deck.

"Hungry?" he said. It was the first he'd spoken in the last twenty minutes. She had started to worry.

"Starving."

"I'll make us breakfast. Waffles sound good?"

"Sounds amazing."

They entered the house. Alexa was feeling grimy and was desperate for a shower. She kicked off her flip-flops and followed him into the great room on bare feet. "Well, this wasn't a very productive fishing trip," she said with manufactured joviality. "We have nothing to show for it."

He darted a look her way. "Better luck next time?"

"There won't be a next time." She headed up the

stairs, her back stiff. "I've crossed it off my list and now I'm done with it. Isn't that my MO?"

"Hey." He moved to the foot of the stairs. "Did I upset you?"

Alexa slowed to a stop. She gripped the rail but did not turn around. "If I had feelings, sure. Since you've concluded I don't…"

"I never said that."

"You didn't have to."

"Look at me."

She turned to face him. His brown eyes held the universe.

He climbed a step and stopped, hesitant. "This means something to me. I wouldn't have invited you here if it didn't. It doesn't matter how long it lasts. The memory is going to stay with me forever. We can't botch this."

Every day, this man revealed a new layer. He was nothing like the person she'd imagined. Alexa had to do away with all the crap she'd projected onto him, do away with the boy who lived in her imagination, if she were to have any chance at getting to know the man before her now.

"It already means something. Jackson, *you* mean something to me."

The faintest of smiles curled his lips. "I make you feel things."

"You do." She did not want to botch this, either. If he wanted to slow down, they would. "Now go and make me breakfast."

Twelve

After breakfast, Jackson left Alexa on the back porch with her laptop and a stack of books. He walked over to the neighbor's house. Earlier, he'd noticed their truck parked out front. If he did not go over to say hello, they'd show up at his doorstep with a crate of produce from their garden or a freshly baked pie. They'd likely turn up at the most inopportune time, like when he and Alexa were kissing in a messy kitchen with mouths filled with whipped cream. It was anyone's guess how they'd managed to sit for breakfast just now.

Loretta Baker came to the door. The petite Black woman in her sixties had the long limbs of a lifelong dancer. She used to wear her silver hair long. Recently, she'd cut it short to the scalp. She greeted him with a wide smile, then called out to her husband. "Honey, it's little Jack."

There was nothing Jackson could do to get Loretta to acknowledge that he was a grown man and not the boy she'd first met. For decades, the Bakers and the Stroms had been the only Black homeowners for miles around. Even though that was no longer the case, the bond between the families was strong.

She motioned for Jackson to come inside. "It's insanely hot. I swear this planet is going to spontaneously combust."

She led him into the kitchen and, without asking, poured him a glass of lemonade. Her husband, Raymond, joined them. Where she was lean, he was round and soft, and appeared to be five years Loretta's senior even though they were exactly the same age.

"When did you guys drive up?" Jackson asked.

"Last night," Raymond replied. "We noticed your lights were on and were going to stop by today, but—"

"But we see you have a very special guest," Loretta interrupted.

"How did you see that?"

"You took her out on the lake this morning."

"Right." Damn! They were good.

"Is that the Lattimore girl?" Loretta asked. "The lawyer?"

"She's not a girl. I'm not a boy. We're both adults."

Ray slapped the countertop. "I bet!"

"She's an old friend."

"Uh-huh." Loretta said. "The Lattimores are in a bind. They stand to lose the oil under their land. Has she mentioned it?"

"We're here to relax," Jackson replied.

He was only beginning to appreciate the amount of stress Alexa was under. His role was to relieve her of it.

"That's right," Ray said. "You two just relax. Forget the outside world."

Loretta nodded approvingly. "She's very pretty, favors her mother. Have you met Barbara Lattimore?"

Jackson tried changing the subject. "I see you've worked on the fence. Looks good."

Ray launched into a review of every company from which he'd obtained a free quote. This bought Jackson some time. He finished his lemonade. The older man would have to pause for a breath at some point. He would make up an excuse to leave.

Jackson was itching to get back to Alexa. He would miss her when they got back to town and had to part ways. No more drawn-out lunches, spontaneous swims or even late-night dance parties. He would miss her like crazy when she returned to Florida. So why was he stalling? For the first time in his life, he was asking a woman to take it slow. What did it matter if it didn't work out? When had he ever worried about that? Sometimes, his love affairs did not last the night. Other times, they stretched out for years. He'd always recovered. Jackson sensed this time would be different. He would not recover so easily. When you get what you want, what you've always wanted, losing it was a devastating blow.

"Anyway," Raymond was saying, "it turned out beautifully."

"Not just the fence," Loretta said. "The deck, too. Just in time for tomorrow's barbecue."

"We're celebrating our thirty-fifth anniversary," Raymond said.

Jackson let out a low whistle. "Congratulations. You two lovebirds make it look easy."

Loretta reached for her husband's hand. "It's easy when you're with the right person."

"You and Ms. Lattimore should come by," Raymond said. "Tomorrow at five."

"We sent an invitation to your parents," Loretta said. "They couldn't make it out this weekend, but you're here. It would mean so much if you would come."

Jackson wasn't sure if he could submit Alexa to the Bakers' intense scrutiny. "I'll let you know."

"You do that." Loretta slipped an arm around his and led him to the foyer. She had impeccable timing and understood intuitively that the visit had come to its natural end. She opened the front door. "One more thing about the Lattimores."

Jackson didn't want to hear it, whatever it was.

"Oil or no, they're a well-respected and powerful family."

"I know that, Lo."

"Okay, well, don't sleep on it."

"What does that mean?"

"It means the girl is a catch. And from what I hear, she's single. You'd make her a fine husband."

"Is that right?"

"Oh, yes." She patted his shoulder this time. "You're a smart boy. Play your cards right."

It stormed later that night. Jackson and Alexa sat facing each other across a travel-sized chessboard. The pawns were tiny and felt like toy soldiers in his hands. They passed a bowl of warm popcorn back and forth while they studied the board. It was Alexa's turn, but she seemed distracted.

"Before I forget," he said, "my neighbors are celebrating their thirty-fifth wedding anniversary tomorrow with a barbecue. We're invited but if you're not up to it, we don't have to go."

She advanced her knight. "I'd love to go."

He moved his bishop without thought. As always, when it came to her, he did not have a winning strategy. "You don't have to."

"I want to."

"If I remember right, barbecues are not your thing."

"I've acquired a taste for it. You think there'll be ribs?"

"I know it."

"Let's go," she said. "Unless *you* don't want to."

Jackson leaned back in the well-loved leather armchair, cradling the bowl of popcorn to his chest. "There's something you should know."

She studied the board, but she was faking. He knew when she was engaged in something, and this wasn't it. "What's that?"

"My neighbors got it in their mind that I'd make you an excellent trophy husband."

A giggle bubbled up inside of her. "What?"

"You heard me."

The rain was slapping against the windows, but all Jackson heard was her melodious laugh. "I always knew you were out of my league," he said. "But damn."

"The position is open, you know," she said.

"Really?" He munched on popcorn, taking his time. "Didn't know you were recruiting."

"You know what they say—behind every great woman is a man with great abs."

"Glad you noticed," he said. "I put in the work."

"And you make good pancakes."

"Waffles," he corrected. "My pancakes are dry."

"Your coffee isn't bad."

"And I'm good with my hands."

"I wouldn't know." She drummed the wood table-top with her fingertips. Her dark-coffee hair was wavy and loose. He had never seen her quite like this, happy and relaxed. "You've yet to demonstrate these skills."

He winked and popped a popcorn into his mouth.

"If it helps to rebuild your self-esteem, Layla thinks you're a catch."

"Layla G.?"

"Uh-huh," she said. "She ranks you among Royal's most eligible bachelors."

Jackson made a face. "Please don't tell me she used those words."

"No." She reached for her glass of wine and sipped. "I believe her exact words were 'He's a catch.' She wants me to catch you."

"Love that girl."

"You *are* that most elusive creature—young, hand-some, single, successful. Why hasn't anyone tied you down?"

"I'm more cautious since starting my own business," he replied. "I've learned to take calculated risks."

"Really?"

They locked eyes. Jackson nodded. "I need…some-thing."

"Collateral?"

"Skin in the game."

She swirled the wine in her glass. "I didn't peg you for one to play it safe."

"Not safe," he said. "Smart."

Jackson wanted something from Alexa, some reassurance that she would take him seriously. If it didn't work out between them, fine. He could live with that. But it wouldn't be because they hadn't tried.

Alexa returned her attention to the board. For a long while, she sat still, calculating her next move. Whether it was with the match or with him, he wasn't quite sure. She extended a hand, letting it hover over the pieces before withdrawing.

"What's the hesitation?" he asked.

"Quiet. I'm thinking."

No one ever made the act of thinking so elegant, so elevated. But if she wouldn't make a move, he would. He was eager to break past this holding pattern.

Alexa picked up her queen and set it down next to his king. It happened so swiftly, he thought he'd imagined it. Jackson was no chess master, but he knew the move didn't make sense. And wasn't that the rookie move she'd accused him of making back in the eighth grade?

"What did you do?" he asked.

She glanced up at him. "I sacrificed my queen."

"May I ask why?" There was no strategic reason to do it, nothing to gain.

"You win," she said. "You were going to win anyway. I'm too distracted tonight. This way is faster."

"But you've robbed me of the thrill."

Alexa did not reply. Her gaze was a caress, and Jackson felt a thrill of another kind.

Thirteen

Jackson was distractingly handsome—sitting across from her, reclined in a battered leather chair, in a loose cotton shirt and faded jeans. Distracted or not, Alexa had the game on lock. She was poised to win but could afford to lose. What better way to drive her point home? She was through with games—not that Jackson had given her any reason to believe that he was playing around. Maybe that was the problem. He was serious, way too serious. That quip about her being out of his league had made her wonder. Would he have been this careful if he were here with another woman, someone less complicated and uptight? Someone not named Lattimore. Or was it their long and storied history? Was it slowing them down?

If that were the case, he had to snap out of it, and preferably in the next hour or so. She was facing another sleepless night. But the way he was looking at her gave her hope. She never felt more beautiful than when pinned by his stare.

He extended a hand. "Come to me."

Alexa launched forward, knocking over the table. The chessboard and pieces scattered onto the Turkish rug. The bowl of popcorn followed. She was on top of him, straddling him, and could confirm to all interested parties that he was very good with his hands. They were everywhere, roaming, exploring. Alexa gripped the hem of his T-shirt and raised it over his head. A moan escaped her when she touched skin. She lowered her lips to his chest and tasted him. A shiver ran through her.

"Let's get rid of this."

He mimicked her gesture, gathering her loose linen dress and lifting it over her head effortlessly. He brought the bundled fabric to his nose and inhaled her scent. She eased it away and leaned forward for him to nestle his nose in the dip of her neck. His hands skimmed the curves of her waist, settling on her hips. She gasped when he dug his fingers into her flesh and drew her closer to him. The rough jeans rubbed her inner thighs. She furiously worked on the button and the zipper. But Jackson was in no particular hurry. He cupped her breasts, delighting in them. He teased one nipple with his mouth and the other with his thumb. Outside, the storm raged. Need sliced through her like lightning.

Alexa pulled away and somehow managed to stand on wobbly legs. She lowered her underwear down over her hips. Jackson protested. "You're doing it again."

She froze. "Doing what?"

"Robbing me of the thrill."

"That's not what I'm doing! I'm trying to get us to the good part."

He reached out and pulled her close. "Alexa," he whispered against her skin, "this is the good part."

It only got better. Jackson sank down to his knees. He inched her silk panties down, slipped a hand between her legs and stroked her with his thumb. He started off gently, then gradually added pressure and speed. Alexa cupped his upturned face and lowered her head to kiss him. He slipped a finger inside her. She tightened around him. Leaning into him, she drove their kiss even deeper. Then, with a sudden growl of impatience, Jackson pulled back, lifted her up and sent her toppling onto the nearby sofa. His wallet and keys were on the coffee table. He grabbed the wallet and rummaged through it until he found the foil packet of a condom. Alexa propped herself up on her elbows. She questioned him with a raised eyebrow.

"Time to get to the good part," he said, kicking off his jeans.

She watched him undress. He was a beautiful man: long and solid, finely sculpted. She could not tear her gaze away.

It had stopped raining at some point. Yet when he stretched out on top of Alexa, a flash of lightning startled her. She wrapped her arms and legs around him.

"Don't worry. I'm here," he whispered against the damp skin of her temple.

Jackson eased inside of her. Finally, they were one, rivals no more. His hands were lost in her hair again. His lips dragged down her throat. She arched her back to welcome him deeper. Pleasure rippled through her, but it was a sudden flash of insight that blew her mind.

She and Jackson had to be two of the most stupid people on earth. All the time wasted antagonizing each
other, baiting each other, and they could have been
doing this. They were lovers at their core, better together than working against each other.

That was her last thought before a thrill took her
under.

At some point, they'd rolled clumsily onto the floor.
Jackson had grabbed a couple of throw pillows and a
blanket off the couch. Alexa pressed her cheek to Jackson's chest, shivering as he stroked her back. Thunder
rolled in the distance. She felt his heartbeat, followed
the slow unwinding of his breath. She was breathing
freely, too—no special app or techniques required. The
house was silent except for the soft rustle of rain-soaked
trees.

Her phone rang. It lay among the scattered popcorn.
She reached for it and checked the caller ID. Two words
flashed on the display: *Office HR.*

"Make it stop," Jackson murmured against her temple. His stubble scraped her skin and sent a shiver of
delight down her spine.

"Sorry. It's my office. I have to take the call."

His arms circled tighter around her. "This late on a
Saturday?"

"Justice doesn't sleep," she said. "Don't get up. I'll
take the call upstairs. It won't be long."

Pulling away from his body, his warmth, was hard
to do. For a brief moment, she was tempted to follow
his recommendation and toss the phone out the window
herself. She couldn't. The knots in her stomach warned
her that this was not a casual call.

With her dress pressed to her torso, she raced up the stairs. By the time she reached her room, the phone had stopped ringing. She dialed the number and fell backward into her bed. As she waited for an answer, she wondered if Jackson would join her here tonight or ask her to his room.

The receptionist answered. "The Law Offices of Anderson and Carmichael. This is Patricia. How may I direct your call?"

Alexa had joined Anderson and Carmichael—A & C for short—just two years ago with the goal of making partner in the coming year. That plan was falling apart, crumbling under her every step. The quality of her work was excellent. There was no doubt about that. However, the interpersonal relationships had her caught in a bind. For one thing, she had never warmed up to the senior partners...or the other way around. Either way, their interactions remained cool, and they kept their distance.

"Hello, Patricia," she said. "It's Alexandra Lattimore. I missed a call. Who's in this late?"

Patricia was the long-standing receptionist who practically lived in the office. Some of Alexa's colleagues called her "Patty Cake," which she seemed to enjoy. Alexa had never dared. It was taxing enough to refrain from addressing the older woman as "ma'am." Her upbringing had instilled in her a stiff formality that she couldn't shake.

"It's been a while. How are you?"

Patricia's tone was gentle. She was the firm's mother hen. Her desk was a designated safe space where employees could stop by for coffee and vent or pick up a little gossip. She kept a well-stocked coffee bar behind her desk and served American roast in the mornings and espresso with pound cake or chocolate between 1:00 and 2:00 p.m. Her nickname was well deserved.

"I'm well," Alexa said. "You know…visiting family."

"Does Arthur know?" she asked.

That was a funny question. Arthur Garrett was the head of the HR department. "Of course he knows. I'm on a leave of absence."

"He left me a note asking me to reach out and ask how long you planned on staying away."

"One month," Alexa said. "Arthur knows this."

Arthur had been the one to suggest she take time off.

"Hey now! Don't shoot the messenger."

There was a slight edge to Patricia's voice. Alexa settled down. She was aware of her reputation at the firm. Rigid. Demanding. Exacting. Once, in the elevator, she'd heard someone whisper, "Troublemaker." The only thing she'd demanded was respect. It seemed that was too much to ask. The average law firm remained the last refuge of the classic boys' club, but A & C was worse.

Alexa did not understand it. She had come to the firm with high hopes. A string of bitter New York winters had forced her to seek a warmer climate. Well before a headhunter reached out with a partner-track position in Miami, she'd studied and passed the Florida bar. She hadn't realized her mistake until it was too late. The senior partners of the firm had little interest in her. She'd recruited clients and won cases. They'd praise her work in staff meetings, reward her with a bonus and go on ignoring her.

Early on, a fellow attorney had invited her to lunch and asked how she was getting on. His name was Theo

Redmond. Alexa had quickly gathered that he was the golden boy of the firm. Every office had one: the tall, blond and handsome type who might've failed the bar a few times and still managed to land at a top firm. Theo was trading on his looks and his pedigree. Alexa didn't mind it, certain that in the end, the legal profession valued substance over style. She'd been wrong.

That afternoon, Theo ordered cocktails and encouraged her to open up to him. "I know how you feel," he said. She was sure that he didn't. "They can be such a cold bunch."

"Aren't you dating Carmichael's daughter?"

Theo was in with the in crowd, and everybody knew it. Things seemed serious with him and the daughter of one of the firm's most senior partners. She was young and pretty and seemed poised to move up the ranks.

"*Dating* is a strong word," he said with a coy smile. "We're involved."

"Well, I'm not involved with anyone," she mocked. "I don't have that privilege."

"You could, if you were...open to it."

Was he suggesting she sleep with Carmichael himself? Before she could ask, Theo had placed a hand on her knee under the table. It lay there, like a dead fish, until she sat up straight and shifted her knees away from him. Not one to take a subtle hint, Theo had later pinned her to the rough concrete wall in the public parking lot and kissed her. His mouth was hot and tasted rank of black truffle sauce. She pushed him away and warned him never to try that again. Except he had tried, again and again, once when they'd found themselves alone in an elevator and another time by the vending machine where she routinely purchased a midmorning granola bar to tide her over until lunch. She'd avoided him, but he knew where to find her. At her wit's end, she'd visited HR and filed an official complaint with Arthur Garrett. Her encounters with Theo abruptly came to an end. She could finally get back to the business of winning cases and cashing her bonus checks. Yet one afternoon, she found herself alone in the elevator with Carmichael's daughter. The woman gave her the dirtiest look. A pit formed in Alexa's stomach. She knew it wasn't over. She'd been naive to think so.

The following week, she was removed from a committee. The week after, she was dropped as second chair from a major trial case in which Theo was third chair. That had prompted another trip to HR. "This is starting to look like retaliation."

Alexa had the firepower to strike back. Her family name had weight and her connections extended far, but she refused to call in favors. She was a professional. She could handle this on her own. Even if she'd asked her father to call on a junior congressman or another, what good could that do? This was a delicate situation. Even a Lattimore couldn't snatch victory out of the jaw of every single defeat.

Arthur Garrett stood from behind his imposing desk. "Cool down, Alexa. Don't toss that word about."

"I'm not the one who needs to cool down," Alexa said. "I've done nothing wrong."

"It's my job to put out fires. Let me do my job."

"What do you suggest?"

"Take some well-deserved time off," he said. "While you're away, I'll meet with the others and get to the bottom of this."

His suggestion was ill-advised but well timed. Her

family wanted her home to spearhead the legal defense against Heath Thurston's claim on their property's oil rights. Instead of flying home for short visits, she could be home longer.

"I'll go," she said. "Only because my family needs me right now. I'll take a month."

Arthur brightened. "It's a win-win!"

That wasn't true—not even close. Something inside her cried out at the injustice of it all.

Alexa regretted having left New York for Florida. Her last firm had worked her to the bone, but they'd valued her efforts. It was very much an ironclad boys' club, but there were a few powerful women at the table, and she'd always been treated with respect.

Anger and frustration formed a knot in her chest. Never had she felt so impotent. She could quit. She could just walk out. Starting over again at yet another firm didn't appeal to her. She'd left New York before making partner. If she didn't stick it out at A & C, her résumé would start to look thin. The best thing to do was to keep taking high profile cases, keep winning and building on her successes until she was recruited elsewhere. That didn't mean she had to suffer in silence in Miami. A & C had four offices nationwide, including one in Dallas. Alexa had never considered transferring to Texas. She had never before wanted to be that close to home. Things were different now. She had an added incentive to consider returning to her home state.

Fourteen

In the time it took for Alexa to wrap up her call, Jackson had swept up the popcorn, straightened out the living room, put on a moody jazz record, and splashed whiskey into tumbler glasses. She came down the stairs and accepted a drink with a shy smile. "Thanks. I needed that."

"Tough phone call?"

"Not really. Confusing more than anything else."

"Want to talk about it?"

She smiled at him over the rim of the glass. "I can't think of anything I'd enjoy less."

"I'm your friend, Alexa." It occurred to him that she might not have too much experience in the friendship department. Maybe she needed a primer. "You can talk to me."

"Technically, we're more than friends." There was a soft purr to her voice. "And we've talked enough."

Her playful teasing was a distraction; he knew it damn well. Jackson wanted to keep on asking questions until he hit the bedrock of truth. Why had a shadow of worry passed over her face when she'd picked up her phone? Why was it necessary to lock herself in her bedroom to take a simple work call? And why was she trying so hard to stonewall him now?

Alexa was looking at him with a pleasantly blank expression, just waiting for him to fold. She took another sip from her glass and swiped at a bead of whiskey on her full lower lip with her pink tongue. Without too much thought, he reached out and cupped her jaw, bringing her in for a kiss. She let the glass skid onto the counter and threaded her arms around his neck. Jackson pulled away and studied her pretty face. Her expression was open; the cool mask had fallen away. He grazed her jawline with his fingertips, silently imploring her to open up to him. Her brown eyes glazed with tears. It was enough to send him reeling.

Something was very wrong. Alexa was struggling under a tremendous weight. Initially, he'd thought it had something to do with her family's legal troubles. Now he wasn't so sure. But as she'd said, they were much more than friends. He did not need to badger her. The truth would come. It was rising to the surface now. He trusted that she would confide in him at the right time.

Jackson kissed her again, this time with ferocious urgency. He was in his boxers and, earlier, she had slipped on her dress to better slip away from him. Jackson tugged it over her head again and sent it flying. She hopped onto a nearby barstool and drew him close. He trailed kisses down her throat, all the while whispering against her warm skin, "No more hiding from me."

She took his face between her hands. "I'm not. I promise. Things are just…messy now."

"Messy? In what way?"

"Work stuff," she said. "Nothing to worry about."

"Then why do you look so—"

She silenced him with a kiss. "Make me forget."

He could do that for her, take her to the brink of pleasure and erase the last half hour from her mind. He could do it handily, but it would only be a temporary fix. Jackson would not leave it at that. He would find a way to ease her burden and rid her of her troubles for good.

It took only a minute to grab a condom off the coffee table. He was soon back in her arms, but it seemed like too long a separation. She wrapped her legs around his waist and repeated her request in his ear. "Make me forget."

Jackson buried himself inside her. The contours of her body were familiar to him now, but the sensation that spread through him was new. They moved at a frenetic pace, pushing each other to new heights—as they'd always done. He tangled his fingers in her hair. Her name slipped from his lips. "Alexa…"

They climaxed together and clung to each other as passion swept through them. Jackson closed his eyes and pressed his forehead to hers. Their sharp intakes of breath softened, then synchronized. She swept her hands down his back. Their bodies were slick with sweat. They'd been rolling on the floor and other places. They needed a warm shower and a warm bed. Jackson scooped her up. She laughed freely as he carried her up the stairs.

On Sunday afternoon, Loretta greeted Jackson and Alexa at the door. Actually, she nearly knocked Jackson out of her way to get to Alexa. "Don't just stand there! Come in! Come in!"

Alexa presented her with a bottle of wine, a gift picked up at the last minute. She'd refused to show up empty-handed. Loretta smiled approvingly and made eyes with Jackson, reminding him of her earlier advice. *Play your cards right.*

Dinner was served on picnic tables set up on the grass. There were ribs. Also, there were champagne cocktails, lobster salad, fresh corn and mini lemon-custard pies topped with the number 35 in gold.

"That's a long time to commit to anything." Alexa frowned down at her mini lemon custard.

"I wouldn't mind it."

She arched a brow. "Should I refresh your memory, sir? In previous statements, you asserted with no ambiguity that you were in no hurry to get married. The record is clear."

Jackson folded his arms and nodded, considering. "I don't deny it. However, I would like to amend the record to reflect my desire to marry eventually and reach a significant milestone, if not thirty-five than twenty-five will do."

"Ah," she said solemnly. "The amendment is recorded and certified."

"Seriously, though," he continued. "I would like something like this. It's nice. Celebrating a lifetime with your love in a home you created, together with good food and good friends. I can't think of anything better."

Alexa just looked at him, wide-eyed. Her curls caught the light of the afternoon sun, and her brown skin had a golden glow to it. She was so beautiful. He wanted to kiss her, but not here. Too many nosy people around.

"You must think I'm some country boy," he murmured.

She reached under the picnic table to squeeze his hand. "You're no country boy, Jackson. You're a successful entrepreneur and one of the smartest people I know."

"I'm a country boy at heart."

"I love your heart, so I guess it's okay."

Those words washed over him. Without thinking, he reached into the pocket of his jeans for a green velvet pouch. While in town that morning, a necklace on display in the window of a vintage shop had caught his eye. He wasn't one to buy jewelry on a whim, but he had instantly thought of her and wanted her to have it.

"What's that?" she said.

He struggled a minute with the ties before emptying the pouch into his cupped hand. She took his hand in hers for a closer look at the gold charm on a thin necklace. It was a miniature chess piece.

"A queen?"

"The most powerful piece in the game."

Alexa's face softened, but only for a second. "It's about time you recognized my greatness." She plucked the necklace from his palm and held it up.

"Like it?"

He was desperate for her to like it, to like *him*. He wanted to please her, challenge her, fight her battles and keep her safe. He had never felt this way about anyone. It made him swoon. It made him giddy. But it freaked him out. This was the sort of thing that only worked out if two people felt the same way. It was no good on its own.

Alexa did not answer his question. Instead, she gathered her hair to one side and asked him to fasten the necklace around her neck. Afterward, he let his fingertips graze her nape. She leaned forward and kissed him, right there, in front of everyone.

A live band set on a podium started to play a blues favorite. Couples poured onto the dance floor and swayed under a canopy of string lights. Above them, a quarter moon peeked through the last tuft of clouds still visible in the evening sky.

Alexa turned to him. "Do you sometimes wonder about the woman who fell through the podium at the TCC pool party?"

The question came out of nowhere. Jackson tossed his head back and laughed. "Sorry to say, I don't."

"She has a solid personal injury claim."

"If you ever want to start chasing ambulances, let me know. I'll hook you up with an ad firm, and we'll tape a few commercials. Maybe erect a few billboards on the highway."

"It's just…everything about that day was so surreal."

"Finding you there was the biggest shock of all. Everything else pales."

"I felt so awkward and out of place until you showed up," she said. "If I could book your services for all future TCC engagements, that would be great."

He took her hand to his lips and pressed a kiss on her curled fingers. "I'm only just a phone call away."

"I may take you up on that."

If you only would, Jackson thought.

"What about the woman who professed her undying

love for your brother?" he asked, doing his part to keep the conversation light.

"I tried to get him to talk about it, but he stonewalled me. I'm not giving up, though."

"Report back when you do."

"If you don't ask me to dance soon, our host is going to poke you with his grill tongs."

Jackson stood and bowed low, a hand on his heart. "Ma'am, will you do me the honors?"

"No, thanks! I'm good."

"Alexa!"

"Just kidding!" She slipped her hand in his. "Take me for a spin, country boy."

They swirled around the dance floor. They danced as the other guests watched them and laughed at the most brazen, the ones who couldn't help but point and stare. She whispered into his ear, "This is odd. We're not the guests of honor, so why do they care? Are you some kind of celebrity in these parts?"

"No, beautiful," he said. "You're the star."

Fifteen

They walked home under a cloudy night sky, hand in hand, gravel crunching under their feet. Alexa was dreaming of the night ahead. Before leaving for the neighbors' anniversary barbecue, they'd made sure they had a quart of ice cream stashed in the freezer for "later." If it rained, they'd put on a record and stretch out on the couch. If the weather held, Jackson would light a fire. She might even try her hand at s'mores.

They rounded a bend and walked up the driveway. The porch light was on, and it cast a glow on the painted-brick facade. The cat stretched out on the porch step was a stray. He gave them the once-over and slinked off. While Jackson unlocked the front door, Alexa noticed that the plants in the flower bed looked limp. She'd snap a photo in the morning and send it to her mother. Barbara would know what to do.

Alexa followed Jackson into the house, wondering who she'd become in these few short days. Apparently, she was the sort of person who sought out her mother for gardening tips. She would have never guessed it.

Jackson locked the door behind them. "We should pack."

Those three words fell at her feet and nearly tripped her. He caught her by the elbow. "Are you okay?"

"I'm fine."

Alexa had forgotten they were heading back to Royal in the morning. The dream was over.

Jackson switched on a few lights. The room glowed. They'd had their first real conversation at the kitchen island and their first dance on the living room floor. They'd made love for the first time on the soft leather couch. She did not want to leave this place—not this soon.

Jackson circled back to find her leaning against the locked door. "What's the matter?" he asked. "Do you need me to carry you upstairs again?"

Alexa felt as if she might burst. "I don't want to go."

"Go where? Up to our room?"

"I don't want to go home," she said. "Let's stay here a few more days."

Jackson did not say a word. Alexa panicked. How could she fix this? Play it off as a joke? She let out a shaky laugh, but it died down within seconds.

Jackson's expression was serious. "You want to stay…*here*?"

She nodded, her throat tight. She must have started playing with the golden chess piece pendent at the base of her neck, because he nudged her fingers away and planted a kiss there. A torrent of butterflies filled her chest.

"You want to stay here with *me*," he said.

Alexa nodded again. "Just, you know, tossing it out there."

His shoulders relaxed. Only then did she appreciate how much tension he'd been carrying. He'd wanted her to enjoy the weekend and would have been disappointed if she hadn't. "I figured you couldn't get out of here fast enough. I thought for sure you were counting the hours."

"Just the opposite. It's been a nice change of pace."

"Uh-huh."

He stepped back. The growing space between them made her uneasy. She reached for him by a belt loop. "Where are you going?"

"I need a minute to process this," he said. "Just days ago, I had to twist your arm to get you to come out here with me, and now you can't get enough."

"Forget it. I'm going to pack."

"Not so fast." He pressed his hands to the door, bracketing her shoulders, locking her in place. "Let me savor this moment."

In her effort to get away, Alexa banged her head on the door.

"Oh, babe." Jackson cradled the back of her head in the palm of his hand. "Does it hurt?"

It didn't hurt. Instead of crying, she started to laugh. She laughed so hard, tears rolled down her cheeks. Jackson wrapped her in his arms. He likely thought she was coming undone, which wasn't far from the truth.

Alexa couldn't wipe away the tears fast enough. "I'm okay," she said between sharp intakes of breath. "I don't know what's the matter with me."

"Nothing is the matter with you," he said. "If anything, I'm in awe. You're under so much stress and handling it beautifully. Don't worry. We can stay for as long as you like."

"Just a couple more days," she said. "Let's not get crazy."

"Done."

Now that it was settled, Alexa wondered why simply asking for what she wanted—in this case, more time with him—had rattled her to the core. She had a reputation for being demanding, yet she rarely ever made demands of anyone. This was a lifelong habit. In class, she only ever raised her hand to supply answers, never to ask questions or for help. God help her if she'd ever had to make her needs known. And yet, she'd done it with him. She'd asked for more time. Jackson was eager to accommodate her.

Alexa ran her hands along his broad shoulders. "Don't let this go to your head, but I think I like you. I mean, *really* like you."

He cocked his head. "You think? On a scale of one to ten, how confident are you?"

"Seven. Maybe eight."

"I like those numbers."

"How about you?"

"Every action has an equal and opposite reaction."

"God!" she exclaimed with a laugh. "You're taking me back to Mrs. Sanchez's chemistry class."

"Actually, it was Mr. Washington's physics."

"Right," she said. "I've got butterflies in my stomach. I can't think."

He took her hand and placed it over his heart. "Do you feel that?"

His heartbeat was steady and sure. "I do."

"Good," he said. "Because it's yours. All you have to do is take it."

The next morning, while the day was still fresh, Jackson went into town to pick up extra supplies for their extended stay, namely bread, cheese, wine and ground beef for burgers. Alexa snapped a photo of the sad flower beds and went to the back shed to rummage for gardening tools. A moment later, her mother called. She answered the call on speaker and went on rummaging. So far, she'd found a half bag of potting soil and a pair of shears. "Good morning!"

"Alexa, this is your mother."

"I know, Mom."

"Are you all right, darling?"

"Sure. How are you?"

"Are you in a safe space?"

Her mother's voice was spiked with alarm. Alexa straightened up too quickly and wacked her head on an open shelf. A few rusty paint cans rolled off the shelf and fell to the floor with a clamor, undermining her response. "Yes, I'm in a safe space. What kind of question is that?"

Her mother wouldn't drop her line of questions. "Where has Jackson Strom taken you?"

"To his lake cabin. You *know* this, Mother."

"That photo you sent—was that a cry for help?"

"The photo of the *plants*?"

"The *dead* plants."

Okay. This was officially nuts. "Mother! Get yourself together."

"What would you have me think? We don't hear from you for ages, and you send a photo of dead flowers."

"I'm fine, Mom," Alexa said. "The plants are half-dead and I need advice. Should I water them? Prune them? Repot them?"

"Who are you and what have you done with my daughter?"

"Ugh! I'm hanging up."

"You know better than to hang up on me, young lady!" her mother warned. "You can understand if I'm a little disturbed. You've never once showed the slightest interest in gardening."

"I've spent loads of time in your garden this trip, but you wouldn't know. You're never around. You're either at yoga, tai chi or pottery class."

"I'm enjoying my summer!" Barbara Lattimore cried, indignant.

"As am I!"

"That's the issue. I've never known you to enjoy anything."

Alexa massaged her temples. "I regret reaching out to you for help."

"Don't say that! You can always count on my help. I'm never too busy for my oldest daughter. I can power walk and chew gum at the same time."

"All right." Alexa lowered herself onto a wooden footstool. "Tell me how to save the plants. Jackson is the only one in his family who comes out here on a regular basis, but he hasn't touched them. They look a little sad."

"Those are not plants worth saving, my dear. Those are weeds."

"That's not true." Even dried up and wilting, the plants had interesting shapes.

"They're weeds. Pull them up by the roots and get rid of them. Find some hearty perennials and start again."

Well, damn. "Thank you, Mother."

"You're welcome, darling. Now, don't hang up. Your sister is here, and she wants to talk to you."

Caitlyn's voice came through the line, bright and sunny. "How's life in the love shack?"

"It's not a shack. It's a very beautiful lakefront cabin."

"But have you fallen in love yet?"

It was the sort of question that would normally make her throw up her breakfast. Instead, Alexa fell silent, even while she heard her mother and sister cackling like hyenas. They were only poking fun, but the innocent dart hit dead in the bull's eye. Last night, she'd admitted to having feelings, but that was a far cry from love. Had she gone and fallen in love with Jackson? No. Her love for him had always been there, a small seed in her heart. It was growing now under proper care and devotion.

Alexa lowered her head between her knees and took shallow breaths. She had to be careful here. The wrong word, the wrong response, would give too much away. But no response would give away just as much. The best defense was offense. Right? *Here goes nothing.*

"Not everyone is obsessed with love, Caitlyn!"

Alexa cringed. She'd struck the wrong tone. That was over the top.

"Uh-huh," Caitlyn said, unmoved.

Her mother jumped in. "When are you coming back? We are expecting you tonight for dinner."

"We decided to stay a couple more days," she said flatly. "There's no rush, really."

Much better. Detached, slightly bored—that was her baseline. Anything more and she'd come across as unhinged to the women who knew her best. Already, the photo of the dead flowers and/or weeds had been a dead giveaway.

"I'm surprised Jackson doesn't have to come back and—I don't know—run his company," Caitlyn replied.

Alexa wasn't surprised. They'd promised each other to make the most of these few days, forgetting the demands of work or even family obligations. They'd made love the whole night to seal that promise. Of course, her sister didn't need to know that.

"It's a slow workweek."

"Mom thinks he's kidnapped you. Could we switch to video to make sure you're okay?"

"Rather not." Alexa looked around her. She was in a dingy shed that let in no sunlight. They would think for sure that he'd trapped her in a dungeon.

"Mom, should we conference in the guys just in case?"

Caitlyn had whispered the question. Alexa hadn't missed a word. "Don't you dare!"

"Okay, girl. Settle down," her sister cooed, as if she were trying to calm a wild horse. "It's all good. We're family."

Alexa switched topics. "How's Grandpa doing? Has he remembered anything?"

She heard her mother sigh. "Your grandfather is the same—clear as day one moment, partly cloudy the next. He only remembers what he cares to remember."

The weariness in her mother's tone was new. She was

growing tired of this sordid affair. The matter was too important to be swept aside. Maybe the tai chi and the new classes were her way to cope with the stress. If his claim on their property turned out to be valid, Heath Thurston would have the power to upend their lives. In essence, they would lose their life's work. It would upset her mother to no end. It would upset them all.

Alexa sat in the shed long after she'd gotten off the phone with her mother and sister. She turned her mother's words over in her mind. *He only remembers what he cares to remember.* She'd long noticed that her grandfather's memory loss was oddly selective. She didn't know what to make of it. He wouldn't voluntarily withhold information. Right? That would be such a low-down, devious—

The door to the shed flew open, and sunlight splashed in. Alexa squinted and turned away just as Jackson filled the doorway. He stepped inside. "What are you doing in here?"

She held up a small rake. "Looking for gardening tools."

He looked concerned. "If you've found everything you need, I'll help you carry it back."

"No need," she said. "I just got off the phone with my mother. She said there's no salvaging the front flower beds. The plants are good and dead. What's left are weeds."

"I could have told you that." When she didn't budge from the little stool, he said, "Are you that upset about it? I can get a gardener up here."

"Don't bother."

He hunched low before her. "What's really bothering you, darling?"

"This sordid affair with my family's ranch is stressing my mother out. I can't believe I hadn't realized until now. She seemed to be holding up fine. I thought her oblivious, to be honest. But she was only looking for ways to cope."

He took her hands. "And how are you coping?"

Alexa admitted that she'd be glad when she could finally put the whole mess behind her. "I want the whole thing to go away. I know… I know… It's wishful thinking, and that's not what they hired me to do."

"They should not have hired you at all," Jackson said. "The Lattimores and the Grandins can afford to hire outside counsel."

"They wanted someone they could trust, someone wholly invested in the case."

"Pay them right and any lawyer will make the case their top priority," he said. "It's different for you. It's personal. Now you face the prospect of letting your family down. That's not fair."

Alexa nodded. "My mother wouldn't make my favorite Thanksgiving sides ever again. My brothers would likely never let it go. Thank God for Caitlyn. She'll always be on my side."

Caitlyn had been adopted into their clan as an infant. Alexa seldom thought about it. Only today, the rickety doors to her heart were wide open, and a flood of emotions were pouring out. Where would she be without Caitlyn ever pushing her to prioritize love? Most likely she'd be in the same position. She and Jackson seemed destined to link up. Except it was a little sweeter knowing that Caitlyn was rooting for her.

"Alexa. I'm serious."

"Don't be," she said. "I distinctly remember us promising not to let the outside world interfere these next few days. I even promised not to open my laptop or do any work."

"That doesn't mean hiding or pretending everything is okay when they're not."

"I'm not hiding anything!" she blurted. Again, she should've moderated her tone. Jackson gave her a quizzical look. She kissed the space between his brows to ease away the crease there.

"All right," he said. "Now, are we going to get out of this shed, or should I order a picnic lunch?"

"Let's stay and make love on the floor."

"Oh, darling." He cupped her face with one hand. "We'll get tetanus if we do."

"Darn. There goes that fantasy."

"There's a hammock on the south end of the property. That's a fantasy of mine."

"Sounds fun." Lying naked in his arms while swinging lazily in a soft hammock, the breeze teasing their warm bodies. Nothing could be better.

He straightened up and helped her onto her feet. "Let's do it."

"Sure," she said. "But first, lunch."

In the days that followed—six in total—Alexa's life mirrored a dream. On the best days, the August sun bore down on them and bleached the horizon white. There was less fishing, more lazy mornings with books and coffee on the back deck, a ride to town for fresh bread and produce, an afternoon swim, a game of chess with rules made up on the fly, meals prepared while de-

bating the news stories of the day, arguing, more arguing and then settling at the table with glasses of wine to
a meal that bore little resemblance to the recipe pulled
from a local blogger's website. At some point, either before the swim or after lunch, Jackson would look at her
in such a way, she'd drop the book, phone, celery stalk
or whatever was in her hand and go to him. They did
not make love in the hammock. That had turned out to
be a logistical nightmare. Instead, she'd taken him up
to her room. They spent their nights in his bedroom,
which left her bedroom fresh for afternoon naps. They
made love with the windows open, the breeze aided
along by the whirl of a ceiling fan.

It was heaven. Miami could keep its palm trees and
sandy beaches; she'd found heaven in a rustic lakeside
cabin in her home state of Texas. "I never want to leave,"
she let slip one day. They were cooking with the television on to the local news. Jackson was obsessed with
the story of the mayor's missing pet cat, June Bug. The
cat had been reported stolen even though there was little evidence. However, expert reporting had revealed
that June Bug, a Persian, was worth over five thousand
dollars and purchased with public funds. "Catgate" was
an example of public corruption of the highest scale.
Jackson's running commentary had Alexa doubled over
in laughter. He was certain the cat was out to sabotage
the mayor's political career. "How much do you want
to bet she's hiding under the porch?"

Alexa chopped shapely cloves of garlic into shape-
less chunks. "I wouldn't put it past her."

"June Bug is no fool," Jackson said. "She's going
to expose the mayor. When she's done with him, he'll
have no career left."

"I'd love to see it."

"Nixon had tapes. Mayor Callahan has a smart-ass cat."

Alexa set the knife down to wipe at the tears at the corner of her eyes. "Do you think he'd be in this mess if he'd bought a fancy dog?"

"Not a chance." Jackson was munching on the carrots he'd attempted to julienne. "Serves him right."

"I wish I could stay to watch the whole thing unfold." Alexa resumed chopping. "I wish I never had to leave."

Jackson didn't reply. Alexa glanced up to find him staring at her. He reached for the television remote and muted the sound. The house went silent around them. "How long do you plan on staying in Texas?"

Alexa set the knife down again. She sensed that this was serious. "The plan was to stay one month. I'm approaching the halfway mark."

"And then what?"

"I go back to Miami, with short trips back here when I'm needed on the Thurston case."

"And then what?"

She knew what he was asking. It wasn't as if she hadn't agonized over the question. How do you walk away from happiness? There was a time she would not have allowed anyone or anything to interfere with her career. She placed career over everything. Her perspective had since shifted. Firstly, her career was in shambles anyway. Fighting for justice in court while suffering injustice at her workplace made the victories ring hollow. Secondly, she'd witnessed firsthand the pitfalls of placing work over all else. Her grandfather was a cautionary tale. Augustus had managed the family ranch until the age of ninety. Most people looked forward to retirement—not her grandfather. He was praised for his grit. Alexa suspected that underneath his steely determination was a reservoir of fear. Augustus's life was his work, and he didn't know how to live without it.

In the end, he'd been forced to surrender the reins when his failing memory became an issue. That was just four short years ago. Her father ran things now, but he'd had to wait his turn for far longer than reasonable. Alexa knew she had a lot of Augustus in her. She had to be careful not to repeat his mistakes, clinging to work just to avoid life.

"What would you like me to do?" she asked.

He leaned against the kitchen island, arms folded across his chest. He wore a heather-gray T-shirt and a pair of soft sweatpants that she'd figured was his favorite. "I can't ask you to do anything I wouldn't consider myself."

Alexa tried to puzzle out his meaning. He would not consider moving to Florida and therefore thought it unfair to ask her to stay in Texas. Without realizing, she touched the golden queen pendant at her throat. It helped her feel centered. Texas was home. New York, Miami—those places had quickly lost their appeal. She put more effort in staying away from Royal rather than making those new cities home. Life in Royal wasn't perfect. It wasn't all country clubs and barbecues. However, her family was here, her legacy was here and now it seemed the man she loved was rooted here, too.

"We have some things to sort out," she said. "I don't have any answers just now. Will you give me time?"

"I'm not trying to rush you into anything," he said. "I just want you to know that I'm an option."

Alexa moved away from the cutting board and took Jackson's face between her hands. "May I kiss you?"

His eyes went soft. "Do you have to ask?"

"I smell like garlic."

"Your fingers may smell like garlic." He took her hands to his lips and pressed a kiss on her fingertips. "*You* smell like lavender, always."

"And you feel warm and familiar to me. I've never been more comfortable, more myself, with anyone."

He kissed her open palm, slid his lips down to the sensitive side of her wrist, all the while his gaze never left her face.

Alexa knew that look. "We're never going to cook this dish, are we?"

"It's too hot to cook. We can toss the veggies into the composter."

She glanced away at her mashed-up garlic. "That's probably where they belong."

It was too hot to go upstairs. Instead, they grabbed a bottle of rosé, a blanket, a bag of chips and a jar of spinach dip and headed outside.

Come Sunday morning, they locked up the house and were gone.

Sixteen

Jackson swung by a coffee shop on his way to the downtown headquarters of Strom Management. He kept a list of his employees' preferences in his phone. His selection of specialty coffees and breakfast pastries would not disappoint. He had a lot to make up for—coffee might not cut it. After all, he'd disappeared for a week with little-to-no notice, leaving his office manager in charge of daily operations and his associates up to their own devices.

They welcomed him back with catcalls and derision—it was that kind of office.

"Settle down, kids. I bought treats."

The office suite occupied the third floor of an old factory building. There were a few conference rooms, a file room and a break room, but the otherwise open–floor plan meant Jackson could not get to his office without running the obstacle course of his employees' workstations. He went from desk to desk and dropped off a "please forgive me for abandoning you" gift set.

First up: Jo-Ann Lindsey, account specialist.

"Here you go, Jo. A medium latte made with oat milk and two pumps of vanilla."

"You never answered my emails, but hey, thanks, boss."

"Sorry about that. Will a chocolate éclair make up for it?"

"Hand it over."

Next: Matthew Johnson, tech guy.

Jackson delivered a large black coffee. No sugar, no cream. "Here you go, buddy."

"Tell me you watched the game. Tell me that, at least."

"Didn't. Sorry."

"And you think coffee is going to make up for that?"

"No…but coffee *and* a cinnamon roll might do it."

Matt snatched the roll. "This isn't over."

"I didn't think so."

Two down, two to go. Next: Cecily Barns, social media coordinator.

She turned down his croissant and macchiato offering. "I'm on a low-carb diet and off dairy for now."

"Sorry to hear it."

"What can I say? A lot can change in one week."

"Apparently."

His last stop was the office of his office manager, Karla Andrews. She waved him in from behind her cluttered desk. "I'll take Cecily's croissant, too."

"Here you go." Jackson handed over her iced latte

and blueberry muffin, plus the butter croissant. "Good to see some things haven't changed."

"I'm actually glad when you're gone. Much quieter."

"Ouch. Can't you pretend you've missed me?"

"I'll do you one better," Karla said, leaning back in her leather chair. "I hear one of Royal's oldest companies is looking for a PR firm to reshape their image."

"Go on."

Rising from receptionist to office manager, Karla had been with Jackson since day one. She kept the business running like clockwork and never missed an opportunity to help grow the client list. Clever, resourceful and barely twenty-five, she had a double life. After she left the office, she worked at a tattoo parlor down the street.

Karla had his full attention until his phone chimed with a text message.

Alexandra the First: News update: June Bug was found three towns over in an abandoned barn.

Jackson: Good morning to you, too, darling. How was your night?

Alexandra the First: Don't act like you're not obsessed with this story.

Jackson: Weirdly enough, I am. How the hell did she end up so far away?

Alexandra the First: Local authorities suspect foul play. The mayor vows to track the culprits.

Jackson: Wanna bet he stashed that cat. She knows too much.

Alexandra the First: For sure.

Jackson: God I miss you. No one here will appreciate the complexity of Catgate.

Alexandra the First: I'm here for you. All you have to do is call. Now let's get to sexting.

She sent him a selfie. She wore nothing but black Spandex and running shoes. Her hair was gathered in a braided ponytail. Her rich cognac skin was covered in a soft sheen of sweat. Jackson noticed the golden queen pendent gleaming at her throat. She was radiant and sexy. Jackson felt a knot in his throat. He'd been good for her. He hadn't just shown her a good time—he'd taken care of her, nursed and loved her back to her true self. Still, he hadn't dared ask for the thing he wanted most of all. He wanted her to stay—ditch Miami and come back home, come back to him. Logically, he was in no position to make such demands after just a few short days, even if those days had stretched out to eternity. Now he wasn't so sure holding back had been the best strategy. She should know how he felt and decide accordingly.

Jackson: I want to do bad things to you.

Alexandra the First: Hmm... Some other time? Gotta run!

Jackson groaned with frustration as he typed. He'd dropped her off at her family's ranch early yesterday afternoon. He was eager to see her again. Meet me later. After work drinks?

Alexandra the First: So long as I get to pick the spot.

He would meet her anywhere. Not a problem, darling.

Jackson sat grinning at his phone like a teenage fool. Karla cleared her throat. Jackson looked up at her, blinking. He'd forgotten where he was. He had not yet made it to his office. "Karla, have you heard about Catgate?"

"No." She sipped her latte. "Should I have?"

"Look into it. Fascinating stuff."

"Why don't you go ahead and take another week? Your head is not in the game."

He got up and backed out the door. "Don't tempt me. I've got one foot out the door as it is."

Of all the places in Royal, Alexa chose North Cove Park, a scenic nature preserve. A trail that led to a cliff with views of a dome of pink granite in the distance. At sunset, the massive rock glistened and revealed all its colors. In other words, she'd chosen Royal's official make-out point.

Jackson put his Mustang in Park. Good thing it was a convertible, the only appropriate car for an excursion deep into North Cove.

"Really, Alexa?" he said. "Of all the places we could have gone, you chose here."

"I've never been. This is special for me."

"You've *never* been to North Cove?" How was that possible? The camping grounds were a popular school field trip destination. "I'm pretty sure we all came up here in the seventh grade, the eighth, ninth, tenth—"

She gripped his hand and squeezed. "You don't get it. I've never been up here in a car with a guy on a date."

"You've *never* been—"

"No! Get it now?"

"Got it." Jackson released his seat belt, turned and looked her dead in the eye. "You just want to live out all your teenage fantasies with me."

"You started it!" She mirrored his gesture, releasing her seat belt with a snap and twisting in her seat to face him. "Why did you have to take me to the prom?"

"That was a stroke of genius, wasn't it?"

"Yep!"

She looked stylish yet relaxed in a body-skimming halter dress and sandals. Her hair was in the same braided ponytail as earlier. She wore no jewelry except for his queen pendent. As always, he couldn't get over how beautiful she was.

"What else didn't you get around to doing?" he asked. "Let's make a list."

"Really?"

"I'm at your service."

"Let's see… There was prom, dates that ended at North Cove and road trips senior year. We've done all of that. That takes care of it, really."

"What sort of dates? Bowling?"

"Don't even think about it. I'm glad I dodged that."

"How about a movie? We usually came up here on big opening nights. You haven't lived until you've made out in the back row of Royal Adventure Cinemas until your lips are chapped to the score of a blockbuster."

Alexa clapped. "Yes to all of that. I'm down!"

"Let's do the movie this Friday night. I'll pick you up at eight."

"It's a date," she said. "Now, we're going to fool around in your car. Maybe you can give me a hickey."

"Sure. But not a word of this to anyone! I've got a reputation to uphold."

"Not one word."

Jackson winked and reached in the back seat of the car for a cooler. A few ice packs kept everything inside nice and chilled.

"What's that?"

He opened the cooler and showed her the contents: a bottle of champagne and fresh fruit. Alexa let out a soundless cry.

"This is not standard North Cove fare," he said. "Back then, we smuggled beer from home and drank it warm. But there's only so much I'm willing to do to fulfill your fantasies."

"Jackson Strom," she said, "will you go steady with me?"

"Steady? How old are we? You're throwing it back to the 1950s."

"Okay. How about this?" She cleared her throat and started again. "So, hey. Wanna be my BF?"

They were only kidding around, but Jackson was suddenly overcome. Yes, he wanted to be her boyfriend. It was all he'd ever wanted since the ripe age of fifteen.

"Well?" she said. "Don't leave me hanging."

"I think we're ready to take it to the next level."

Her smile widened, more dazzling than pink granite at dusk. "Yeah."

"For sure. I feel this amazing connection between

us," he continued, lifting phrases straight from his high school playbook. "You know what I mean?"

"I do."

"We vibe."

"Totally."

"I'd like to see where this is going."

"I'd like that, too."

"So we're on for a movie on Friday?"

"I'll have to ask my dad, but sure."

"Cool. But we're going to the new dine-in theater." Jackson ripped the foil off the bottle of champagne. "You couldn't pay me to go back to Royal Adventure Cinemas. I have standards now."

"I don't care where we go."

He popped the cork, poured two glasses and proposed a toast. "We're officially high school sweethearts."

"Awesome," Alexa said. "To us!"

He set his glass in the cup holder. "Now, let's make out."

Seventeen

Two days later, Alexa met with private investigator Jonas Shaw. She would rather be sipping champagne with Jackson at sunset, but duty called. Over the past few weeks, Shaw had been following a trail of old money. He'd combed through bank records, notes and ledgers in search for any scrap of information. After weeks of silence, he'd finally reached out. It appeared that he'd found something major. Alexa agreed to meet him at Royal Diner.

Shaw fit his long, wiry frame into the red booth and ordered a black coffee. When that was taken care of, he delivered the unsettling news in his blunt way. "Augustus Lattimore had the properties surveyed for oil."

Alexa was confused. "*Properties.* Plural?"

"Both your family ranch and the Grandin property."

"When?"

"About a year before he signed the oil rights over to Cynthia."

"But why?"

"It's worth knowing if your land is sitting on oil."

"Maybe, but what interest is it of his if the Grandin ranch has oil or not?"

"It's possible the Grandins were looking to sell or strike a deal."

"It's not possible." Alexa stirred sugar in her coffee. "The Grandins would never sell or strike any kind of deal. Neither would my grandfather, for that matter."

Jonas ran his long, thin fingers through his salt-and-pepper hair. "The paper trail tells a different story. Try filling in the blanks. Sit your grandfather down and ask—"

"That's a waste of time," Alexa interrupted. "His memory is slipping."

Shaw nodded gravely. "My mother is the same. Still, she has her moments. Flashes of lucidity. It's like a light bulb will go off in her head. Keep trying."

"Sure."

If a light bulb went off in Augustus's head, he'd flip the switch and turn it off. When it came to this matter, it appeared he preferred to leave things in the dark. She wasn't comfortable discussing this with a stranger or even Layla. Wouldn't Layla suspect the worst if it were proved Augustus was withholding information? Maybe she could confide in Jackson?

Since they got back from the lake, they'd been spending all their free time together. Jackson was fun and easy to talk to. She couldn't imagine being away from him for too long or resuming her life as before. Late last night, she'd settled on a working solution: the Dallas office. Jackson's business wasn't portable. His contacts and network were local. He couldn't afford to uproot and start over elsewhere. She, on the other hand, was eligible for admission to the Texas Bar by reciprocity and employed by a firm with offices nationwide, including a location in Dallas. They'd be carrying on long distance, but the distance would be manageable. There was no reason to stay in Miami. Things hadn't worked out as hoped. Rather than remain there and waste energy trying to sort things out or put out fires, she would walk away.

"Having your property surveyed for oil is standard practice," Jonas said. "But it's a bit odd to lump in your neighbor's property while you're at it. It tells me that Lattimore and Grandin were working together, plain and simple. Probably went in for a two-for-one type deal with the surveyor. Augustus and Victor Senior were best friends, so maybe that explains it?"

"I'd like to see the surveyor's report."

"So would I, but it can't be found. That's why it has taken me so long to get in touch with updates. I've been searching."

Alexa pushed away her coffee cup, scraping the linoleum tabletop. Archeologists had better luck unearthing the secrets of ancient tombs than they'd had with this case.

"Now, settle down," Jonas said. "I have a lead."

"You do? Let's hear it."

"Does the name Sylvia Stewart ring any bells?"

The name was familiar. For years, she and Caitlyn had been tasked with helping their mother assemble gift baskets for the office employees. Sylvia Stewart was top of the list. Every year, her mother made sure to stuff her basket with her favorite Belgian chocolates.

"She worked with my grandfather."

"Correct. She was his secretary at the time and handled your grandfather's paperwork and the like. If anyone can shine a light on this, it would be her."

Alexa brightened. "That sounds promising."

"Not so fast," Jonas said. "She's retired now and an active world traveler. It's taking a while to track her down."

"Great."

She reached for her cup. It was back to waiting, then. What was she supposed to do in the meantime? Just sit around? Well, maybe not… This might be the perfect time for a quick trip to Miami. She could speak with HR and put in a formal request for a transfer.

"I know we're in the weeds now, but things will turn around," Jonas said. "They always do."

Shaw insisted on paying for the coffees. Alexa watched him leave the diner and walk briskly across the street. Dusk was settling. All at once, the streetlights flashed on. Alexa's coffee had gone cold, and still she lingered at the table. She thought it best to update her siblings and Layla on the progress of the case right away and schedule a formal meeting with the Lattimores and the Grandins in the morning. As usual, her father would get her mother up to speed, or not. It wasn't clear her mother wanted to be in the loop.

She slipped her phone out of her purse and tapped on the group chat for her siblings. It had last been updated with a series of hilarious memes and cat videos. Her next contribution to the chat was not so upbeat.

She hated to be a downer, but that was her assigned role in her family.

Alexa's phone to Lattimore4thewin: Just a quick update, guys. It seems granddad had the ranch and the Grandins' lots surveyed prior to assigning away the oil/mineral rights.

After a pause, the responses poured in:

Caitlyn: Why would he do that? I'm so confused.

Jayden: That man was up to something. I just know it.

Jonathan: He probably had his reasons. Have you tried asking him?

Alexa: Uh...no, actually. Wonder why I hadn't thought of that?

Caitlyn: That's sarcasm. BTW.

Jayden: I know it when I hear it.

Caitlyn: Alexa is doing all she can.

Alexa: I've done everything except lock him in a room and cuff him to a table.

Caitlyn: No need to go there.

Jayden: Why not? I'm willing to try.

Jonathan: I'm on a call with a supplier. Will catch up with y'all later. Good work, Alexa. Thanks for keeping us informed.

Caitlyn: Dev says hi…and good night.

Jayden: Hold up! Are we seriously not going to discuss Alexa's hickey?!

Alexa flushed. She slipped the phone back in her purse and stood to leave. All the while, the hated device buzzed and buzzed.

Alexa returned home and sought out her grandfather. After an early dinner, her grandmother told her he had retreated to his study. She found him in his worn leather recliner, a glass of liquor in hand. He was listening to a recording of an old bluegrass concert. Augustus had worked hard his whole life and hadn't devoted much time to recreation. Alexa wondered if this was his way of catching up.

He greeted her as if he hadn't seen her in days. They'd gone on their usual walk just this morning. "Come in, Alexa. It's good to see you."

She moved a pile of books off an ottoman and sat down. "Good to see you, too."

"What brings you around?"

"I had a conversation with Jonas Shaw."

"Who's that?"

Alexa took a breath before responding. Her words came out in a dry monotone. "The private investigator we hired to look into Heath Thurston's claim to the oil under our land."

"Ah. Right."

"He has evidence that you had our land *and* the Grandins' ranch surveyed for oil and other minerals."

Her grandfather straightened up in his recliner. "I'm sure I did no such thing."

Alexa suppressed the urge to cross-examine her grandfather. *Sir, under penalty of perjury, is it your testimony that you did not have the land surveyed?*

"Are you sure? He has receipts."

"I don't care what he has!" he snapped.

Alexa caught a glimpse of the powerful man that he once was. But she had a lot of Augustus in her, and she didn't cower easily. She reached for the sound system's remote control and cut the volume. "Nothing happened on this ranch without your knowledge and approval. Now answer the question. Did you or did you not have the properties surveyed?"

Augustus averted his eyes. "I don't know. I'm not sure, dammit!"

"Grandpa, this isn't a minor thing."

There was one more thing that bothered Alexa. Her grandfather was a shrewd businessman. She didn't believe for one minute that he'd sit on a resource that could potentially make him millions. Neither would the late Victor Grandin. Everyone would have her believe that they went to the trouble to have the properties surveyed just for kicks? It didn't make sense.

"Ask Victor. He'll remember," he said.

Alexa softened. Maybe that was enough cross-examination for tonight. Augustus didn't remember Victor was dead. Or maybe he knew Victor was dead and couldn't answer? Argh! She could start again in the morning. She pressed the mute button on the remote, and music poured out of the speakers embedded in the walls. "What are you drinking?"

"Nothing but the finest whiskey from Tennessee."

She got up and went to the liquor cabinet. There was ice in a bucket and a crystal decanter filled with amber liquid. She poured herself a nightcap.

Eighteen

Jackson had no idea which movie they'd just sat through. It was a foreign film with subtitles, but that wasn't the issue. The bluesy score had set the right mood. He'd kept Alexa close to him with a hand tucked under her soft blouse. They kissed straight through the end credits—every kiss deeper, messier—until the theater lights cut on.

Squinting, she pulled away from him and smoothed her clothes. "How do I look?"

"Delicious."

"Come on," she said. "Let's get out of here."

They left the theater and found his car in the garage. Jackson leaned against the hood, and she stepped into the space between his legs. They hadn't discussed how the night would end. Since their return to town, she'd spent her nights at home. They'd talked on the phone for hours as if they really were back in high school. It was fun and all, but he didn't want to go back to that tonight.

"Want to get a coffee?" he asked.

She rubbed her smooth cheek against his stubble. He loved it when she did that. "I don't know. It depends."

"On what?"

"On whether you have an espresso machine at your place."

Jackson laughed. They were always on the same page. "As a matter of fact, I've got a top-of-the-line espresso machine."

"Is that right?" She dragged a finger down his jaw. "Does it froth milk?"

"I can't say for sure. But it has all the bells and whistles."

She made a face. "You don't know how to use it?"

"I've never touched the thing," he confessed. "There's a coffee shop just steps away from my building, and they get all my money. I believe in supporting small businesses."

Alexa's mouth twitched as she fought back a smile. "Small businesses are the backbone of our economy."

"That's what I always say."

She shrugged. "I don't need coffee, just an excuse to see your place."

"You don't need an excuse, either. I've been dropping hints all week."

"It's been an odd week," she said. "I had a tough meeting with the PI on our case, followed by an even tougher meeting with the two families. I suspect my grandfather is withholding information, but I don't know if it's on purpose or if he can't access the information because of the dementia." She waved her hands before her face as if to wipe away her last statements from an imaginary whiteboard. "Never mind all that. I'm killing the mood."

Jackson cupped her face and drew circles on her cheeks with his thumbs. "I don't want a mood. I only want what's real."

She rested her head on his chest. "This feels real to me."

He wrapped her in his arms. "Let me tell you about my week."

"Okay."

"When I wasn't busy responding to a week's worth of emails, I've been thinking about making love to you in my bed. It's killing me."

Alexa nodded. "Same here."

"Really? My bed, not yours?"

"Mine still has the same floral bedspread my grandmother gave me when I was fifteen. It's not the vibe."

"My bed it is! Let's go."

He moved to hold the passenger door open for her. Just before slipping in, she paused to kiss him. "We've exhausted my list of unfulfilled teen fantasies."

"Already?" he said. "Don't cut it short on my account. I'm down for it."

"I didn't have much of an imagination back then," she said. "Don't look so disappointed. Now we can move on to other things."

"What things?"

"This whole experiment has been one-sided, don't you think? I figure we could make some of your wishes come true."

He was down for that, too. So much so, he was glad the open passenger door was wedged between them. He kissed her and whispered into her mouth. "Alexa, get in the car."

He switched on the light in his foyer. Alexa immediately cut it off. There was enough moonlight pouring in from the wall of windows in his living room to light the way. Moonlight touched every reflective surface, making the everyday appliances sparkle. He'd lived in this condo for three years, and it had never taken on this magical, dreamy quality. Alexa made everything special. She'd made an ordinary stay at the lake cabin into something grand, a memory that would never fade in his mind. He had a feeling that tonight would mark him as well, and he was ready for it.

She dropped her purse onto the console table. "You can give me the grand tour in the morning."

"Before or after a coffee run?"

"We'll work out the logistics later." She kicked off her heels and ventured into his space and reached the spiral stairs that lead to the loft. "Up here, I'm guessing?"

She'd guessed wrong. The upper level was command central. It housed his home office and the huge TV reserved exclusively for sports. It was a chaotic mess. His bedroom was on the main floor, hidden from view by pocket doors. Jackson went over and slid the doors open. She approached, but he stepped in her way.

"This is my fantasy," he said. "I should run things."

"You know… I'm beginning to think your ultimate fantasy is beating me at chess."

Jackson did not disagree. "That's high on the list,

but we can leave it for tomorrow," he said. "Tonight, I want you to do exactly what you're told."

Her eyes raked over his face. He could tell she was teetering between caution and curiosity. "I don't know about that."

"I suggest you make up your mind."

Surrendering control was not something that she was predisposed to do, but Jackson had a suspicion she was aching to do it. The weight of the world was on her shoulders. Surrendering was the easiest way to unburden herself.

"How do I know you're not going to do something crazy?" she asked. "Like cuff me to a bedpost?"

Actually, that sounded kind of fun. "Is that really so crazy?"

"Okay. Bad example."

"You won't know either way. That's part of the thrill."

"For you, maybe."

He leaned against the doorframe. "For you, too. I promise."

"All right. What do you want me to do?"

"Undress."

She glared at him. "Out here?"

"Why not?" It wasn't as if they were out in the lobby.

Alexa squared her shoulders and raised her chin. He geared himself up for some major pushback. Instead, their standoff lasted all of two seconds. She reached for the zipper of her jeans, yanked it down and stepped out of them. Her willingness to play along was ushering in a new era. They were no longer locked in an endless power struggle. They'd moved past all that. Even so, he read a silent promise in her eyes to make him pay for everything she allowed him to get away with tonight. That was his Alexa.

He watched as she stripped away her silky blouse and underthings. When she stood before him, naked, Jackson had to ball his hands into fists to keep from touching her.

He stepped aside to let her through.

Alexa's breath caught when she took in his wide custom bed. The headboard was upholstered in Belgian linen. He couldn't tie her to it if he wanted to.

"It's beautiful."

Jackson unbuttoned his shirt. "Thank you."

"So…" She turned to him. "What do you want from me?"

Only Alexa could make that question sound like a command.

Jackson tossed his clothes, and they landed in the heap just outside his door. He slid it shut. "Now you tell me what you want."

She arched a brow. "I'm not sure that's how this game is played."

"Do you want me to lick you, touch you, bite you…? Tell me. What do you want?"

Alexa's brown eyes glowed hot. She caught two fingertips between her teeth and just stared at him.

"Don't tell me you're at a loss for words."

She could not, under any circumstances, back down from a challenge. He knew that about her.

"I want your mouth all over me."

"All over? Or a more focused exploration?"

"Jackson! Stop making me wait."

"Get in bed."

With a sigh of relief, she fell onto her back with her

arms outstretched over her head. She was magnificent. Jackson could not hold back. He explored her with his mouth, his hands, sucked and licked her until her back arched with pleasure. A jagged sigh escaped her. "God! I've missed this."

It had only been a few days, but those days were too long. He had missed this, too. It had been all he could do to keep from driving to her house in the middle of the night.

There were condoms in each drawer of the bedside tables. He grabbed one and she helped him with it. Then he slipped a hand between her legs to bring her right back to the brink of pleasure. Alexa twisted and moaned and whispered, "I don't want this to end."

Those words swirled in his mind as he made love to her. He didn't want this to end, either. If they were on the same page on this as well, there was hope for them yet.

Later, when they collapsed in each other's arms, happiness grew wild inside of him. If he had Alexa, he had everything.

Her breathing steadied and Jackson was sure that she'd fallen asleep. He nestled closer, burying his nose in the nape of her neck. Alexa spoke up in the dark.

"Jackson?"

"Yes, babe?"

"I'm leaving for Miami soon."

Nineteen

Arguably, Alexa's timing was awful. Jackson pulled away from her and rolled onto his back. She immediately suffered withdrawal and cuddled closer to him, looped a leg over his to keep him at her side. "Don't worry," she said. "It's not for long. I'll be back in a few days."

"Why do you have to go at all? You just got here."

"I have some things I'd like to take care of."

"Like what?"

Alexa eased away from him. She sat up and drew her knees to her chest. This was the moment to come clean. As in chess, she tried to envision how this would play out. Step one: tell Jackson that she'd been sexually harassed at work. Step two: urge him to trust her to take care of the matter herself. Step three: request that he keep the whole sordid affair a secret. In three moves, she could ruin their night.

She started rambling. "You know how it is. Demanding clients need reassuring. The firm represents some major players. Owen Black & Co., Southbound Airlines, ETT, Blue Moon Beer—"

"ETT?"

"Evergreen Tractors and Tailors."

"We've done work for them. Southbound, too."

"What a small world!"

"Those companies are incorporated in Texas."

"That's right. And so are you."

She leaned over and kissed the tip of his nose, hoping they could put the awkwardness behind them. He slipped a hand under the sheets. His fingers lingered on her waist, but his hold on her was firm.

"Basically, what you're saying is that you could handle the bulk of your work from Texas."

There was no putting anything past Jackson. She was heading back to Florida to officially request a transfer. It was settled in her mind. It wasn't as easy as packing up her things. The request might take months to get approved. She would have to tie a lot of loose ends with her Florida-based clients. She was willing to go through the trouble. It was worth it. Jackson was worth it. However, she did not want to get his hopes up. She would share the good news with him once the transfer was approved and she had an office set up in the Dallas location.

"Who knows?" she said evasively. "Maybe someday, I will."

Jackson's expression clouded. "Are you sure you have to go back?"

"Yes, I'm sure! We don't all have the luxury of being

our own bosses. Some of us have to report back to the office from time to time. It's not unusual."

"Are you sure you're not just putting distance between us for the sake of putting distance between us?"

Alexa's heart fell. That was the last thing she wanted. Being with him felt so natural, and yet it was never boring. Each day brought a new thrill. No one got her like he did. No one had ever tried. She was not going to jeopardize this.

Instead of saying any of this, she made a joke. "What if I promised to bring you back key lime pie?"

Jackson closed his eyes. Her chest tightened in response. All her emotions were compressed inside her. Alexa wanted to reassure him, but she couldn't open up without her secrets popping out.

She stretched out over him, propped her chin on his chest. Her nose brushed against his trim beard. "Does it feel like I want to put distance between us?" He looked at her through thick lashes. His mouth was pressed into a hard line. She reached up and traced a finger along its curve. "Well, does it?"

"Sometimes I can't read you."

This was when most people would say, "I'm an open book." But she wasn't. She was an ancient text locked in a display case. She was exhausting. It was time she clean up her messes before he gave up on her.

Alexa sought out her brother Jonathan when she returned home late the next morning. He was at the barn. She found him by the back gate, overseeing the delivery of organic fertilizer. "There you are! I looked all over for you."

He straightened up. With the black Stetson, he was

even taller and more imposing than usual. No wonder women were intimidated by him. He whipped off his gloves and approached her with long, confident strides. "Is anything wrong?"

"Nothing is wrong," she said. "I need a favor. Could you give me a ride to the airport on Monday?"

Earlier that morning, while Jackson was on a coffee run, Alexa purchased the airline ticket online. She had no intention of dwelling in Miami. After meeting with the head of HR and checking in with her supervising attorney, she would head out for a shopping spree. Apart from a few sundresses, her wardrobe was pretty basic and utilitarian. If she and Jackson were going to carry on as they were, she needed fun and flirty outfits and tons of lingerie.

"You're leaving? Where are you off to?"

"Back to Miami for a couple of days. I have some business to take care of. Work stuff. You won't even notice I'm gone. Jonas Shaw is still coming up empty, so I have a few free days before I'm needed back here."

"Bet you Jackson will notice."

"Jackson will be fine. He's a strong man."

"That might be true, but he is weak in the knees for you."

Alexa peered up at him, shielding her eyes from the sun with a hand. "You're a love guru now? Let's talk about you and Natalie Hastings."

"There's nothing to talk about."

"You sure about that? Have you reached out to her?"

"No need."

No need? Alexa couldn't believe her oldest brother—the good one, the serious one, the favorite by all regards—was acting like this. At the very least, he should call the woman and clear the air. It was the gentlemanly thing to do. She was probably mortified. Even their recalcitrant private investigator had had the grace to look her in the eye and deliver crappy news in person and over coffee.

"Don't leave her twisting in the wind," Alexa scolded. "You're better than that. Ask her out for a drink. Even if it doesn't amount to anything, you'll give her a chance to laugh it off."

Jonathan rolled his shoulders back, a sure sign that he had reached peak frustration. "It won't amount to anything, so why bother?"

"Who's to say?"

"I say! I'm not interested in anything."

"Do you hear yourself? Sounds to me you're not interested in living your life. You're too young, too smart and too good-looking to live like this!"

She was hollering now. The ranch hands had definitely heard her. They tossed curious glances their way. Alexa took her brother by the arm and marched him up the brick path back to the main residence. She decided that he needed a break.

Jonathan came along, walking stiffly beside her, grumbling all the way. "I expect this kind of talk from Caitlyn, not you."

"Caitlyn was brave enough to fight for her happiness. There's a lot we can learn from her."

Jonathan stopped dead in his tracks. "What has Jackson done to you?"

"Never mind Jackson. This is about you."

"Well, I'm fine."

"No, you're not. You're dodging and deflecting." Alexa didn't stop there. "You're burying yourself in work to avoid life. You're still hurting and, possibly, still hung up on the past."

Jonathan had married young. He'd barely been out of college, still in his early twenties, and was not yet ready for marriage. Alexa hadn't approved of that blessed union. She wore a scowl in every single wedding photo. So much so, she'd been edited out of the wedding video. The marriage failed, which came as no surprise to her. Her former sister-in-law hadn't been ready for marriage, either. Anne was pretty but also needy, clingy and sort of whiny. Alexa had not thought her a good match for her Jonathan. It had been difficult watching her older brother, her idol, use all his energy to placate his young wife. She privately rejoiced when their divorce was finalized. Jonathan did not. He took it hard. He'd failed at something meaningful and at such a young age. It had marked him. Ever since, he'd buried himself in work. Someday he would take over the ranch. He was the heir apparent. That didn't mean he had to devote himself to this land like Augustus had.

Jonathan removed his hat and looked up to the sky. He was probably praying for restraint. She poked him in the ribs. "Did you know Natalie had a crush on you all this time?"

"Crush? Are we back in high school?"

Point taken. Not everyone wanted to throw it back to freshman year like she and Jackson had. Having said that, Jonathan was deflecting once again. "Very well. I'll rephrase that." Alexa cleared her throat. "Mr. Lattimore, at the time of the public disclosure of Ms. Hastings's feelings toward you, were you or were you not aware of said feelings?"

"What was that, Counselor? Could you repeat the question?"

"Just answer me!"

Jonathan was laughing. Alexa had succeeded at something. She'd made her oh-so-serious brother laugh. His answer, though, made her sad.

"Natalie doesn't have a crush on me. She doesn't know me."

"You live in the same small town. Of course she knows you."

"She only thinks she does."

"Hmm… How can I say this without hurting your feelings?" She looped her arm through his and continued along the path. "You're being a patronizing ass."

"Alexa, I know what I'm talking about."

"Your hidden depths are pretty shallow, Jonathan. She took a look at you and sized you up. It probably took her all of five minutes."

They passed the bench where she and her grandfather sat for their morning chats, passed her mother's rose garden and newly installed terrazzo birdbath, and climbed the steps to the back porch. From there, they had a view of the neighboring ranch. The roof of the Grandin home peeked out from beyond a tuft of oak trees. She anguished over all that they stood to lose. Alexa did not know how much she loved her home until that moment. Suddenly, even Dallas seemed too far, too distant a place. The truth sparked in her heart. She'd been gone too long. She wanted to come home.

Alexa turned away from her brother. She did not want him to see her in her emotional state. As it turned out, Jonathan couldn't get away from her fast enough.

He yanked open the screen door. "I'll take you to the airport. Send me your flight info."

"Sure. Meanwhile, you'll think about what I said?"

His grip tightened on the doorknob. "I'm not going to call her, Alexa."

Alexa raised her hands in surrender. Was there anything more stubborn than a Lattimore? Jonathan was an adult, and she couldn't force him to do anything he didn't want to do.

"I've known about Natalie's *crush* for a while now," he continued. "We've crossed paths a few times, and there's always been sparks."

Sparks? What a bombshell revelation this was! For once in her life, she wished she could conference in her siblings. She had to get Jonathan on the record.

"Sparks fade sooner or later."

"Not always!"

"In my case, they do."

"You don't know that."

"I know me."

"So do I. And I think you're talking crazy. Any woman would be lucky to have you." He gave her a pointed look. "Well, any woman except the one you married. She was an enigma inside a riddle, and honestly, I'll never understand her."

"I'll never understand women, period."

"One bad marriage doesn't disqualify you from the Love Olympics. You've got to get back up on the balance beam and try again. The sooner you move on from the past, the better."

"I *have* moved on!" Jonathan cried out. "Life is good now. *I'm* good. And I'm not going down that path again. The sooner you all get that, the better."

Alexa remained impassive in the face of her brother's outburst. She'd drop it for now. Later, she'd come at it from another angle. But she couldn't let him have the last word. "Give love a second chance, Jonathan."

Her brother shut the door and leaned against it with folded arms. "Give love a second chance?"

"It's a cheesy line, I know." She'd officially joined the ranks of people who said sappy things in the name of love. Heaven help her. "Just open your heart and give love a second chance, okay? I promise you won't regret it."

"Oh yeah?" He narrowed his eyes, studying her. "How can you be so sure?"

"I'm not sure of anything. It may not work out. That doesn't mean you don't try."

Jonathan let out a low whistle. "Jackson must have done a number on you for you to be talking this way."

"Oh, shut up!" Alexa pushed past him, yanked open the screen door and entered the house. Jonathan's big-hearted laughter bounced off the walls and followed her inside.

Miami welcomed Alexa home with a torrential downpour. She was lucky her plane was able to land. Her neighborhood was flooded. The taxi driver refused to drop her off at her building, and she ruined a pair of three-hundred-dollar shoes trekking one block in ankle-deep water. She caught a glimpse of herself in the mirrored elevator and recoiled. She looked like a drenched poodle. She felt wretched. The dark clouds that blocked the sun made her feel unwanted. And for whatever reason, she hated everything about her home. The rented condo had a hotel vibe, which she'd loved up until a day ago. Jackson's bedroom had been a heavenly re-treat. He'd hired a designer to achieve that dreamy look. Meanwhile, Alexa had moved into her fully furnished space over a year ago and had yet to add a houseplant.

Alexa peeled off her destroyed designer ballerina flats and left them in the foyer with her travel bag. In the living room, she fell back on the stiff leather sofa and took in the rain-blurred views framed by the wall of windows. Jackson had timidly offered to travel with her. She had declined, mostly because she felt bad that he'd lost so much time at work because of her. He shouldn't have to disrupt his entire life. That was the reason why she'd gotten her brother to take her to the airport. Besides, she could handle this on her own. Still, she missed him. She would have liked to get his take on her impersonal space. The couch would be so much more inviting with him stretched out on it.

Their last conversation came back to her. He'd texted her late last night. Alexa was pouring a bath when she'd heard her phone chime with the message. Because of the nature of her work, her phone was always within arm's reach. He'd sent her a selfie. He was at the office, catching up on work, and was scruffier than usual. She shivered at the memory of those soft hairs scratching the skin between her breasts. And then there was the trail his lips forged when he had dragged them from her knee to the tip of her toes.

A message followed. Admit you'll miss me.

She immediately typed a reply. I miss you right now.

He called her. The phone rang in her hand, and she answered without a second's hesitation. "Hey, you."

"Hey," he said. "If I were insecure—"

"Which you're not, obviously."

"Not at all."

His voice was gruff with fatigue, but how she loved it! He was preparing for a meeting with a big client that he'd neglected, partly because she'd taken up so much of his time. "Go on. I didn't mean to interrupt."

"If I were insecure, I'd think you were skipping town when things were getting good between us."

"Hmm... That would make me a coward."

"Or human."

Alexa sat on the edge of the claw-foot tub. She turned off the faucet and cut the water so she could hear him better. Her thoughts bubbled up in the silence that followed. "This is good, this thing between us. Isn't it?"

"Honestly?"

"Yes."

"You're the lover I've been waiting for."

She closed her eyes. More than anything, she wanted to reassure him. It might not seem like it, but she was running toward him, not away. There were too many strings tying her to Miami. She had to snip them loose.

"Alexa, are you still there?"

"When I come back, we'll discuss the future. We have more options than you know."

When Jackson didn't respond right away, Alexa bent forward and pressed her head against the cool, wet subway tile. She hadn't meant to come across as a college recruiter. Could this really be what he'd been waiting for? A woman so locked up in herself, she broke down at every turn?

"Is that so?" he said, finally. "Enlighten me. What are these options?"

"You'll know more when I get back," she said.

"You're going to have to trust me on this. Can you do that?"

"I trust you, darling."

A lump formed in her throat. Alexa couldn't believe it. At long last, she was pulling first in a race that actually mattered to her.

"Good night," he said. "And don't forget my key lime pie."

The next morning, Alexa was staring at the same water-stained view, only this time from a slightly different angle and from much higher up. She lived three blocks away from her office building, which gave her a short commute—a rare luxury in Miami. Arthur Garrett had agreed to a meeting. She was ushered into the HR director's office without delay but was kept waiting a good quarter hour. First, he took a call; then another, saying only, "I see," and "I understand," while staring blankly at an open file on his desk. Alexa studied her cuticles and tapped her foot. She wanted to jump out the window.

When he finally ended the call, he was pink around the ears and looked as if he had a lot to say. Alexa didn't want to hear any of it—not the hollow apology for having kept her waiting or the phony interest in her welfare. With her back ramrod straight, she raised her hand the way she did in school when she demanded a professor's attention. "I'm here to formally request a transfer to our Dallas office. Any time is fine, but the sooner the better. I want to be closer to my family."

Arthur leaned back in his massive leather chair. The wall behind him was entirely glass. He looked as if he were tipping into the bay. "Ms. Lattimore, I regret to say we cannot accept your request."

Alexa's hand dropped onto her lap. "I beg your pardon?"

"Your request is denied."

Arthur Garrett was a practical man who lacked vision. Alexa would have to draw him a picture. "A good number of our clients are based in Texas. With my contacts, my family's contacts, I can easily draw in more."

"The answer is still no."

Alexa's stomach had gone sour. He was enjoying this. His thin lips were straining back a smile. She was the one who lacked vision here. There was something else at play, and she didn't see it.

"Any reason why?" she asked. "I've done good work for this firm. My record speaks for itself. There's no reason I can't continue to be an asset in Dallas."

"If we believed that, we'd rush it through. Unfortunately, we don't."

We *are going to lose our shit.* "I don't understand."

"I'll explain." Arthur joined his fingertips in a steeple. "There was a time we could count on you to deliver. Not anymore. Your commitment to the firm is in question."

Alexa could not muster a word. Outrage clamped her throat. Arthur took advantage to press the intercom. He let his assistant know that he was ready. Ready for what? Alexa wasn't sure. She was reeling. Her head was foggy. Although this was the absolute wrong time to indulge in an existential crisis, there was no fighting it. She'd been the golden girl, the one to beat, the best of the best, and on and on, forever! She had never been demoted, passed over for a plum promotion or, heaven help her, fired. That was what was happening. She had no doubt.

The door swung open, and Richard Carmichael walked in. Actually, he sailed in. He wore a navy suit and a wolfish smile. His tan was a shade of terra-cotta more suited to pottery. His teeth gleamed white. "Alexandra, it's been a while."

"Not that long. I'm on leave and visiting family." She awarded herself bonus points for managing to sound coherent.

"Ah, yes. Meanwhile, the rest of us are hard at work."

"I don't understand. Arthur approved my leave."

"I urged you to take some time off because you were not having the best time," Arthur said. "A couple of days at most."

Not having the best time? He had to be kidding her. Alexa labored to get a grip on herself before she lost it. *Breathe in. Breathe out.* Negotiations were over. *Breathe in. Breathe out.* She needed a cool head for battle.

"Richard, Arthur, we're all busy people. If you have something you want to say to me, I would appreciate a direct approach."

Arthur cleared his throat. "We understand you have other priorities now. A transfer to Dallas won't solve the problem."

"What other priorities? I've always put my clients first."

"You're a fine attorney," Richard said. "No one is disputing that. We wouldn't have recruited you otherwise. But it has to be said—you are no longer one hundred percent committed to this firm. We expect our attorneys to work as a team, quash petty squabbles, keep the firm's best interest first place."

"You're firing me because I lodged a complaint against Theo Redmond."

"You're not fired, Alexandra."

Now she was more confused than ever. "Then what are we doing here?"

"We're asking for your resignation," Richard said. "It's simpler that way."

"Like this, you'll be free to pursue employment opportunities in Dallas or wherever life takes you," Arthur added.

Alexa was trembling with rage. Hot tears stung her eyes. She would rather die than break down here. She was a Lattimore, Royal born and bred. These men would not take her down. It was time to end this game. "I had such high hopes when I took this job. A & C had a stellar reputation. I was flattered when you recruited me. God, you had me fooled. Theo Redmond is a walking liability. You know this, and yet you've chosen to let go of a *stellar* attorney to placate a lazy and frankly useless one—or worse, to please the senior partner's daughter. It's embarrassing."

"You're blowing this out of proportion," Arthur stammered.

"Am I? Let's see what my friends at the Equal Employment Opportunity Commission have to say about that."

Richard Carmichael settled in the chair next to hers. He crossed his legs and made a grand show of appearing unruffled. The taut muscles of his neck told a different story. "Go ahead," he said. "Go make some noise at the EEOC. You may have some resources and a few contacts back in Texas. We have the full force of the fifth-largest law offices in the Southeast. We can drag this out for years."

Alexa felt for the golden pendent underneath her silk blouse and was instantly calmed. The moment called for a tactical move. She wasn't sure she wanted to pursue legal action. It was well known that Richard Carmichael planned on retiring in eighteen months. He would be off living his best life in Nantucket while she was languishing in the court system. It would trash her reputation and might jeopardize her career. But she couldn't let them off so easily. Some way or another, they would pay. Right now, though, she wanted nothing more than to get as far away as possible from these two men, this toxic office and this city that held nothing more for her.

Twenty

"There's just something about the way she picked up and left. It's a work trip. I know. I get it. No one works harder than me. But there's something going on there. She's hiding something. I can feel it."

"Have you asked her what's going on?"

"She won't answer a direct question. It's driving me nuts."

"Sounds like there's a communication gap. If it's making you uncomfortable, you have to address it."

"I don't want to come off as clingy. I'm not that guy. I respect boundaries."

"There's no way to build a healthy relationship without solid communication. I understand she's not as open as you'd like. But you have to learn to make your needs known. You talk about respecting the boundaries of others and that's good. However, you have to teach others to respect you. If you're coming into a new, budding relationship with an open heart, it's not too much to ask for your partner to do the same. Does that make sense to you?"

Jackson sat up on the bench on which he'd been reclining. It made all the sense in the world. He was walking on eggshells around Alexa, afraid to do or say anything to upset her. And it was only because he wanted her so badly. That approach wasn't going to work. It was making him feel a little desperate and a lot insecure.

"It does. Thanks for seeing me last minute."

"Absolutely, dude. You're a valued client." Russell, his lumberjack of a personal trainer, had been holding a plank position the entire time. He hopped onto his feet and slapped Jackson on the back. "Now, that's enough talk. Fifty push-ups. Get going. I want to see you work."

Jackson was gathering his equipment, stuffing his gloves and sweat-damp towels into his gym bag, when Russell offered one last bit of advice. "Send her flowers!"

"What kind of basic advice is that?" He sent flowers to his mother on Mother's Day. "My first gift to her was a gold pendant in the shape of a—"

"Flowers!" Russell bellowed. "It never fails. Send a big fat bouquet to her office. She'll melt."

Outside, the sky was thick and heavy. A storm was headed their way. Jackson sprinted back to his car. Once behind the wheel, he scrolled through his phone's contact list. He had the florist on speed dial.

"Mr. Strom, good to hear from you. What can I do for you today?"

"I'd like to send a bouquet of roses to Miami."

"Very nice. We are running a special on white roses."

"Not interested." He was only interested in long-stem, red-hot I-can't-wait-to-get-you-naked roses. "That's not the vibe we're going for."

"I recommend Obsession. Gorgeous crimson blooms."

"Sounds right."

"I recommend three dozen."

"Send me the bill."

"The address?"

"Hold on." He hit the browser icon and searched for Alexa's law firm. He read the address to the florist.

"I'll need a suite number. Do you have one?"

"I can give you the name of the office building."

"Not enough. You won't believe how many people with the same names work in the same buildings. Next thing you know, the wrong person walks away with your gorgeous flowers. You don't want that."

"No, I don't," Jackson said. "Give me a minute."

He switched lines and called the Law Offices of Anderson and Carmichael. A woman answered with a giddy tilt to her voice. Jackson wondered if he had the wrong number until she said the name of the firm. "How may I direct your call?"

"Hello, my name is Jackson Strom. I'm looking to mail a package to my attorney, Alexandra Lattimore. I need a suite number to ensure the documents get into the right hands."

"I'm sorry to inform you that Ms. Lattimore is no longer a member of A & C."

"I'm sorry... What?"

"Ms. Lattimore has parted ways with the firm."

"As of when?"

"As of now."

Jackson gripped the steering wheel. The car was parked in the lot behind Russell's gym, and still he felt as if he were crashing. "Could you...tell me why?"

"That's confidential, sir."

Jackson was sweating again. Why would she quit her job and not tell him? Was that what she'd gone off to do? He drew in a long breath. The air around him had gone stale, and he stifled a cough. Back when they were in school, whenever he was going up against her, he would try to think as she would to anticipate her next move and to gain a competitive edge. Alexa had quit her job. Why? To come home and give them a chance? Hardly. That was wishful thinking, at best. As much as he would have loved it, Alexa was not impulsive or rash. She wouldn't upend her career for his handsome face. What was it, then? What was he missing?

"I don't know who will handle Ms. Lattimore's cases," the receptionist continued. "If you're willing to hold, I can find out."

"That won't be necessary. This was a sensitive matter."

"I should transfer your call to a senior attorney, anyway," she said. "If only to advise you on your options."

He didn't want to speak to any other attorney. Still, he managed to control his voice and lean hard on his southern accent. It always worked like a charm. "I'm just gutted, you understand? Ms. Lattimore has an impeccable reputation. She came highly recommended. I knew I was in capable hands. Any hint on where she'll be heading next?"

The receptionist huffed. "She doesn't have a good reputation around here."

"Is that right?"

"Uh-huh," she whispered. "She's something of a troublemaker. Trust me on this, you dodged a bullet with that one."

And there it was: the missing piece. He'd been right this whole fucking time. Something had been eating at her. He knew it. He knew she wasn't okay. He'd assumed her family's legal troubles were the root of the problem and had not dug further. Things had gone south at work. Okay. Fine. Shit happens all day. Why hadn't she confided in him?

By the time he'd gotten off the phone with Miami, he'd forgotten all about the flowers. The florist called him back, and he arranged for the roses to be delivered to her home in Royal instead.

"I got news!" Karla called out from her desk when he got back to his office.

Jackson strode past her door. "Not now!"

The benefits of the workout had faded. He was fuming. *She's something of a troublemaker.* The words chased after him like angry bees. Alexa was a genius, an ace. They were lucky to have her. They should have put her in charge of the whole place. What kind of shortsighted, narrow-minded, backward people was she working with? He was going to find out.

Karla trotted after him. "Sorry. This can't wait."

Jackson fell into his desk chair and fired up the computer. "What is it?"

Karla hovered in the doorway. "I'll make it short.

Claire Kennedy of Kennedy & Sons has requested a meeting."

Jackson looked up from his computer screen. His fingers hovered over the keyboard. He'd been typing *Anderson and Carmichael* into a search engine. This news was worth the minor interruption in his quest to take down one of the top law offices in the country and avenge the love of his life. And there it was: the thing he'd been dancing around for days. Alexa was the love of his life. He had to protect her.

Although she came from a large family, he knew she often felt alone. She was probably accustomed to fighting her battles alone, too. But that was no longer the case. He was here for her—if she could only learn to rely on him.

"Did you hear me?" Karla snapped. "Claire Kennedy is a big effing deal!"

Claire Kennedy was the heir to a family-owned home-improvement-store empire. In addition, she sat on the board of a few influential nonprofit organizations. If she'd requested a meeting, he would have to jump on it. It was likely she was meeting with the competition as well. "Absolutely. Set it up."

"She suggested a lunch."

"Of course. Anytime she likes."

"More enthusiasm, please."

"Sorry. I'm having a crisis."

"I'll close your door."

He thanked her and apologized again. Jackson sat alone in the quiet space. For the first time in his adult life, his work was no longer his top priority.

He was in love with Alexa.

His pulse steadied and he let the feeling flow through

him. There had never been another woman for him, no
one with such a hold on his heart. She'd been his first
and only love. It was time he proved it.

Twenty-One

Alexa showed up at the door of her childhood home with the entire contents of her condo packed up in four suitcases and three boxes. Their longtime housekeeper, Josie, helped her haul the luggage in from the porch. In a deliberate attempt to delay the moment she'd face her loved ones, Alexa had not bothered to call on her brothers, Jackson, Caitlyn or anyone for a ride from the airport. She'd ordered a ride from a driver with a truck.

Her mother rushed to the door. The look on her face was so comical, Alexa would have burst out laughing if the circumstances weren't so dire. She felt like a loser, and there was no worse feeling in the world.

After she'd stormed out of the meeting with Richard Carmichael and Arthur Garrett, there'd been a humiliating trek down the hall to her office. Every head had turned, but no one met her eyes. The air was electric with gossip. The news had gone around and back. She even heard muffled laughter. There were empty boxes already piled up on her desk. Trembling with rage, Alexa rummaged through her desk drawers for the few personal items she had, stuffed them in her structured tote bag. She exited the office with her head high only to fall apart on the sidewalk.

Jackson kept calling. She was dying to speak with him, but he would know that she'd been crying. There was no way to hide it in her voice. She texted him a string of lies:

Can't talk right now. Still in a meeting.

Heading out to dinner with a coworker. Will call later.

Miss you, but this dinner is running late. I'll call before bed.

She never called. That night, she got busy packing her stuff. She reached out to her landlord and paid the penalty to break the lease. She arranged for the dealer to pick up the sports car she rarely drove. She was done with Miami and vowed not to return for a long time. But now she was back in Royal with no plan, no job, nothing to do except wallow. Just the thought of enlisting a headhunter gave her a headache. She wanted to curl up in bed and cry. And yet, when her mother came to the door, she had to paste a smile on her face.

"What is going on here? I wasn't expecting you until the end of the week."

"Well... Surprise! I'm back."

She carelessly tossed her bulging carry-on suitcase

into the foyer. It bumped up against the marble-top console table. A bouquet of red roses tipped over, and her mother rushed to catch it. "Careful!" she cried. "You'll destroy your flowers."

"Is that for me?"

"Yes! Jackson had it delivered this morning," her mother explained. "You should read the card. It's lovely."

Alexa ruffled through the roses, which were stunning, and found the rectangular envelope with the note addressed to her that her mother had already opened and read.

Alexa, first of my heart, we need to talk.
Patiently waiting.
Love,
Jack

Alexa's vision blurred. She forgot her mother and everything around her. She could feel the pressure of Jackson's hand on the small of her back and the ghost of a kiss under her ear. She reached for the golden queen pendent and pressed it to her lips. Jackson Strom had to be the sweetest man she'd ever known. She strongly doubted he was "patiently" waiting for anything, but it was the thought that counted.

"We have to talk, too," her mother said. She eyed the boxes piled up in the foyer. "Just how long do you plan on staying?"

"Why?" Alexa fished her phone out of the back pocket of her jeans. "Are you planning on converting my bedroom into a yoga studio?"

"Darling, this is your home, and you are always welcome. But you left in a hurry, and now you return with all this *stuff.* You look as if you haven't slept in days... This is the sort of behavior I expect from Jayden, not you."

"Uh-huh." Alexa typed a brief message to Jackson to let him know that she was back and eager to talk. She pocketed the phone. "I live a fast-paced life, Mother. Try to keep up."

"What's your plan, exactly?"

Her mother stood with her hands on her hips, her feet spread wide. She was not going to allow Alexa passage until she gave some sort of an explanation. Alexa blurted the first thing that came to mind. "I'm here to stand by my friends and family. I plan to stay for as long as it takes and see this business with the oil rights to the end. This ranch is my home, and I will defend it tooth and nail."

Her mother did not seem convinced, but she stepped aside and let Josie sweep past and up the stairs, hauling a suitcase. Alexa grabbed a box and followed. Her mother did not pick up a thing and hounded them all the way to the second floor. "Are you sure this has nothing to do with the man who sent those roses?"

"You think I'm going through all this trouble for a man? Does that even sound like me?"

"I wouldn't be against it if it were the case. Jackson Strom grew up to be a fine man with an impeccable reputation. You two would be a perfect match. We could have the wedding right here on the property. But I've never seen you act irrationally. Now is not the time to start."

Here she thought her mother would jump for joy

because she'd finally found "a good man." There truly was no pleasing that woman.

In her bedroom, her mother sat at the window bench while Alexa and Josie made several trips to bring up the rest of the boxes and things. Barbara looked pretty in a pair of linen palazzo pants and a coordinating blouse. She seldom wore makeup, but lately she'd taken to dusting golden-peach blush on her cheeks to brighten up her deep mocha complexion. Alexa had inherited her high cheekbones and, some would say, her imperial air.

Josie arranged the boxes neatly in Alexa's walk-in closet. "All done! I'll find the box cutter and set it aside for you."

"Thanks, Josie."

"It's no bother," she said. "I'm glad to have you back."

"I appreciate that."

"Will you be joining the others for lunch?"

"Others?"

"The whole family is here," her mother replied.

A family lunch on a Wednesday? "What's the occasion?"

"It's Dev's birthday," her mother replied.

"Oh…"

"Everyone is here."

"Oh…"

"Your vocabulary is severely limited."

"It's just that I'm exhausted," she said. "I'll skip it. No one was expecting me, so I won't be missed."

"Nonsense! Come join us for dessert, at least."

"Mom, look at me. I'm a mess."

"Who cares, darling? We're family. And you can explain to everyone why you packed up and fled Florida as if there's a warrant out for your arrest."

Alexa smirked. "Nice."

Her mother stood and smoothed out the wrinkles in her linen pants. Clearly she cared about her own appearance.

Her mother and Josie left, shutting the door behind them. Alexa sank into her ancient four-poster bed and wondered if she should even bother unpacking. How could she possibly live here? If she didn't join the others for lunch, they'd call her antisocial. It didn't matter that she was cranky and sleep deprived. And to top it all, she wasn't even hungry. She'd wolfed down a burrito bowl at the airport between connecting flights.

All Alexa wanted was to speak with Jackson. He would be upset with her for dodging his calls, but she'd decided on the plane to come clean. She would tell him the truth. Not the whole truth, of course—a version of it. He didn't have to know *all* the sordid details. It would just upset him, and for what? There wasn't much he could do. It was better to leave that mess in the past. She was not going to sue A & C. There was no way to go about it discretely. Her family would learn about it and wage a war, seeking to destroy the thirty-year-old law firm. Her mother would never shut up about it. All of Royal would learn how Alexandra Lattimore had not been able to cut it in the big city. Would another firm hire her after that? Did she even want to work for another firm? Maybe it was time she branched out on her own. She had so many decisions to make, all of them equally pressing. For the moment, she had to freshen up and face the firing squad.

Twenty-Two

After some back-and-forth with Claire Kennedy, she and Jackson had agreed to meet for lunch on Wednesday at the Texas Cattleman's Club. Jackson wished he could cancel. He had not heard from Alexa in twenty-four hours and was in no mood to sit through an indulgent three-course executive lunch. Nonetheless, he set out early, hoping to make a good first impression and wrap up the encounter. On the drive to the TCC, a message from Alexa flashed on the dashboard monitor, turning his plans upside down.

Back in town. Thanks for the beautiful flowers. We've so much to talk about. Can't wait to see you.

At the first traffic light, Jackson executed a U-turn and sped down the causeway in the direction of the

Lattimore ranch. So much for making a good first impression… He would rather be late than not check in on Alexa and make sure she was okay.

He arrived at the ranch; several cars were parked in the drive. A housekeeper let him in and asked him to wait in the entryway, where the bouquet of red roses was on display. Raucous conversation and laughter rattled through the house. Jackson realized that he was interrupting a gathering of some sort, but it was too late to duck out. Barbara Lattimore was gliding toward him, arms outstretched.

"Jackson! Welcome!" Mrs. Lattimore cried. "Is this your first time here?"

"Yes, ma'am," he said. "I believe it is. It's lovely."

"Alexa should have invited you ages ago. We'd love to have you for dinner someday."

"Is now a bad time?"

"No, of course not. It's my future son-in-law's birthday. We've cut the cake, so you're right on time."

"I can't stay long."

"Nonsense," Barbara said. "Alexa will be thrilled to see you. You must have put a spell on my daughter, because she's packed up and left wretched Florida in a hurry. Now that she's finally home to stay, we hope to see more of you."

If this was true and Alexa had moved back, it wasn't because of any spell he'd cast. It likely had more to do with her losing her job. Did Barbara Lattimore know? She seemed awfully upbeat. Jackson hadn't even noticed when she looped her arm around his and steered him from the foyer to a formal dining room. Everyone was seated at a large oval table. Jackson recognized the elderly Augustus Lattimore; his wife, Hazel; Alexa's father, Ben; and her siblings, Jonathan, Jayden, Caitlyn and Dev Mallik. Dev was wearing a paper party hat. He waved Jackson in. "Don't be shy. The cake alone is worth venturing into the lion's den."

Barbara scolded Dev. Everyone laughed and ate cake. It made for a heartwarming scene, but where the hell was Alexa?

Someone tapped him from behind. He glanced over his shoulder and there she was. The mix of anger, confusion and hurt that had clouded his head in the last twenty-four hours receded like fog. Alexa looked worn out and frail. Her brown eyes were dull, but he could make them shine again. Her shy, uncertain smile broke his heart. She was still wearing his necklace. He hugged her and kissed her cheek. "I forgot your key lime pie," she said, contrite.

"Don't worry about it. I'm just happy to see you."

He wasn't the only one happy to see her. Judging by her family's reaction, this was her first encounter with them as well. They cheered her arrival. Caitlyn blew her a kiss. Jonathan demanded to know why she hadn't asked for a ride back from the airport. Jayden wondered why she hadn't answered any of his texts.

Ben Lattimore sat staring at Jackson from his seat at the head of the table. It had been a mistake to gloss over him. A distinguished Black man in his sixties, Ben Lattimore was as intimidating as Jackson knew Augustus once was. This was the man that Jackson would have had to reckon with if he had taken Alexa to prom. The fact that he and Alexa were grown didn't seem to make any difference. The rules were the same.

Jackson stepped forward. "Good afternoon, Mr. Lattimore."

He nodded and looked to his daughter. "You left without saying goodbye. Now your mother says you're back to stay."

"I'm back to stay as long as necessary to help with the case."

Jackson flinched at this caveat. What if the issue resolved itself tomorrow? As he understood it, the matter was simple: if the claim on the oil rights was valid, there was nothing more to be done except maybe negotiate a buyout. Although, the word on the street was that Thurston wasn't open to negotiations.

"What about your job?" Her father continued his interrogation, unbothered that he was shredding the party mood. "Don't you have to return at some point?"

"I'm on sabbatical," Alexa said.

She stood ramrod straight, unwavering even as she lied to her father.

"Is that a thing lawyers can do?" Jayden asked. "I thought that was for college professors."

"Yes, Jayden. It is."

"Don't get me wrong," Ben said, "I'm happy to have my daughter back. Just wanting to make sure you're not jeopardizing your career for us."

"Or anyone," her mother added sweetly.

If that barb was meant for Jackson, Barbara Lattimore had it all wrong. Their daughter's career was in jeopardy, but he had nothing to do with it. She certainly hadn't shared any of the details with him. It was comforting to know that he wasn't in the minority. It looked as if Alexa planned on burying this secret in a Florida sinkhole.

"Could I speak to you privately?" he said.

"Sure." Looking relieved, she asked the others not to eat all the cake and led him out by the hand.

In the foyer, she rushed into his arms. Again, the conflicting brew of emotions receded. Jackson was so in love and so confused.

"Let's go to the garden. It's nice out there."

He squeezed her hand. "I can't. I'm already running late for a meeting. I came here just as soon as I got your text."

"Oh, God," she said, pushing him toward the door. "I don't want you to miss out on work because of me. Go to your meeting and come back later. I'll be here."

"Are you okay?" he asked softly.

"I'm fine."

"How did things go in Miami?"

She manufactured a smile. "Not so great."

"That's okay. Tell me what went wrong."

"Just some misunderstanding with HR about my leave."

"A misunderstanding?"

"Yes. It's resolved. I'm back and free to focus on the task at hand."

It hit him from nowhere, a sucker punch to the chin. Alexa wasn't going to confide in him—not now, not ever.

"It's resolved. Really, Alexa?"

"Yes. Really. God, you sound like the others."

"The others want the truth."

She took a step back. "And you? What do you want?"

"Your trust."

She let out a rusty laugh. "You know I trust you! Why not go to your meeting? We can talk—"

"Let me guess," he interrupted. "Later? We'll talk later. Is that what you were going to say?"

Alexa had gone pale. She nodded slowly but did not utter a word.

"And later, we'll push it back to even later still."

"What's your point? I've been busy and—"

"Busy with work? Is that it?"

"Yes, with work." She reached for his hand and tangled their fingers. "There's nothing or no one else. I promise. My job has been so demanding lately and—"

Jackson freed his hand from hers. He wasn't going to let her lie to his face. "Stop, Alexa. When you're ready to talk, *really* talk, come find me."

Her face fell and Jackson, torn apart inside, nearly faltered. He was this close to grabbing her and kissing away the frown lines. If he caved now, any foundation of trust and respect would be eroded. He wanted a future with Alexa. If she wanted him, it was up to her to make the move.

Jackson arrived at the Texas Cattleman's Club ten minutes late for his meeting with Claire Kennedy. Fortunately, Claire showed up even later. She found him at the bar. He had hoped to sneak in a drink to calm down before the meeting. She'd had the same mindset. She slipped onto the bar stool next to him and ordered a whiskey, neat.

"Jackson Strom, I'm having one hell of a day. Sorry to have kept you waiting."

"Not at all," he said. "I'm honored."

"Are you?" She looked at him. "You seem pissed off."

"I'm having one hell of a day, too."

The bartender served her drink. She raised her glass. "Cheers to that."

Jackson liked how this meeting was going. Claire Kennedy was a small woman with silver hair dyed the same shade of blue as her eyes. No matter how dainty her appearance, he should not forget that she was one of Royal's shrewdest power players.

"I had to fire my nephew this morning," she said with a sigh. "My sister is going to hate me. Want to come over to our house for Thanksgiving this year? It's going to be a riot."

Jackson thought of Alexa taking on her family's case. "Working with family isn't easy."

"He was my accountant. The boy didn't know what he was doing. He only went into accounting to please his parents. And now I'm expected to keep him employed to please them, too."

"It's a vicious cycle."

"I don't have time for that. They should have just let the boy be a magician or whatever else he wanted to be."

"How's his sleight of hand?"

"The hell if I know."

Claire was chuckling now. Jackson knew they'd get along great, whether she hired him or not.

"Your turn," she said. "What's bugging you?"

"I'm trying not to mess up a new relationship," he said. "We're at the tipping point. It could go either way."

"Huh. Nice to know love is still alive."

"I guess that's one way to look at it."

"Let's get to the point of this meeting so we can get you out of here. What do you say?"

Jackson liked her more and more. "Let's do it."

She joined her slender, vein-lined hands on the polished bar top. "My stores need a refresh. We hired a fancy architect and did all the work. Way over budget, if you ask me. Still, it's not enough. Our customer base is aging."

Jackson skipped ahead. He knew what she was about to say next. "You want to attract millennials."

"We need to," Claire corrected. "There's no way around it. It's a matter of survival."

Jackson picked up his glass and gave the amber liquor a swirl. Claire Kennedy's dilemma was inherent to all legacy businesses in desperate need of rebranding. The classic big-box stores that dotted the suburbs were dinosaurs in today's marketplace. Most couldn't keep pace with e-retailers. He tried to think about the last time he'd gone to a home-improvement store. It had been with Alexa. They'd driven a half hour from the lake cabin to reach one. She'd picked up perennials and potting soil. She was determined to revive the front flower bed that curved along the porch. The memory of that afternoon resurfaced. He could see her in a white cotton dress, sunglasses and simple leather sandals. He'd pushed the cart and followed her around the nursery. He'd reached for terra-cotta pots off the top shelves and lifted heavy bags of soil off the ground. Later, he loaded it all into the truck. A solid hour had passed, and it had been heaven.

"Plants."

"Excuse me?"

"You want to attract younger customers? Sell them plants."

"We have a garden section."

"I'm not talking daisies here." Alexa had consulted social media to make her selections. She'd had her heart set on exotic blooms, green plants with odd-shaped leaves or even edible flowers. In the end, she'd had to settle for carnations. He'd tried to lift her spirits by pointing out that carnations were, in fact, edible.

Claire's eyes were narrowed in thought. She was probably thinking he was wasting her time. Meanwhile, he was thinking the red roses he'd sent Alexa were a mistake. He should have sent her carnations.

"You might be on to something," she said finally. "My niece's apartment is like a jungle. She calls the plants her babies, her plant babies. And she keeps fussing over them. She's got apps and a special thermometer and everything. Can you believe it?"

"I can," Jackson said. "The question is, can you?"

Claire made a face. "You're saying I should *get over myself* and *get with the times*."

She used air quotes for emphasis. Jackson ignored the sarcasm. "That's exactly what I'm saying."

"I don't get it," Claire admitted. "I never enjoyed gardening. Either that or I never gave it a chance. It was the sort of thing I was meant to do. As a woman, I mean."

He understood very well. A woman of her age had likely spent her life pushing against rigid stereotypes. She'd likely been expected to cook, bake *and* grow her own tomatoes. However, his generation had grown up in a digital world and yearned for contact with nature. "Plants are the antidote to tech. They ground us, in a way."

"I suppose," Claire said. "And now you're going to try to sell me on a full-scale social media campaign."

"You know it. A television ad airing weeknights at six is not gonna cut it, Claire." After a pause, he added, "May I call you Claire?"

"Depends. May I call you Jack?"

"No objections."

"All right, Jack." She was nodding and frowning at the same time. "I like this plan. Once we lure them into our store through the lawn-and-garden department, what's to stop them from looking around?"

"Next thing you know, those crazy kids are buying patio furniture."

Claire cackled. "Jack, you're a charmer."

"I think you've charmed me," Jackson said. "Should I even be giving you all this free advice?"

Claire slapped him on his back. "I can't tell you how to run your business, but in my line of work, giving away free samples is always a good idea."

The bartender returned. This time, he handed Claire a key card. "Your room is ready. Anytime is fine."

She slipped the card into her structured purse. "I booked a private meeting room for a video conference after lunch. My new lawyer is located in Dallas, which is a pain. I should have gone with someone local." She asked the bartender for a menu. "You don't mind if we catch a quick bite here, do you?"

"Not in the slightest."

Jackson didn't have to consult the menu. He ordered his usual TCC special, a burger-and-fries combo. Claire ordered a chicken Caesar salad.

"I'm not going to beat around the bush," Claire said. "You're hired. I want to put you in charge of our social media strategy."

"And maybe your niece could give us some insight."

"We could bring her on as a consultant!" Claire exclaimed. "That'll get my sister off my back. I fired her son but hired her daughter. It balances out."

Jackson raised his glass. "Two birds, one stone."

"Efficient. I love it."

Speaking of efficiency. "If you need to prepare for your next meeting, I'm fine wrapping things up. I can take my lunch to go."

"There's no rush. A & C can wait."

"Anderson and Carmichael?"

"You've heard of them?" Claire said. "Their closest office is in Dallas, which makes dealing with them a hassle. Not sure if I'm going to hire them. They come highly recommended."

A sudden jab of anger had Jackson reaching for his whiskey. "I wouldn't recommend them."

"Why not?"

"I know for a fact they don't treat their people right."

"How do you know?"

Jackson couldn't get into that with a stranger when he hadn't even gotten into it with the person in question. "I'm not at liberty to say."

Claire considered him awhile. She then pulled out her phone and dialed a number. "Jenny, cancel my conference call with A & C," she ordered. "I won't be hiring them. I need someone here in Royal, someone I can talk to face-to-face. That's my style. Also, if you could, contact Raul Perez and Miriam Carver. At last week's dinner, I recommended they reach out to A & C for that thing we're working on. Let them know I've changed my mind about A & C. We'll go with another firm. Thanks, Jenny. Want me to grab you lunch? Uh-huh. Okay." She tucked her phone back in her purse with a satisfied little smirk. "There. Now we can enjoy our lunch."

Jackson liked Claire Kennedy well enough before. Now he straight up worshipped her.

Twenty-Three

Moments after Jackson had stormed out, Alexa stood staring at the closed door. Caitlyn entered the foyer, balancing two slices of cake on their grandmother's best china. "Did I miss Jackson?"

"Uh-huh. He left. He's gone."

Her words tumbled like pearls sprung loose from a broken string.

Caitlyn approached, her delicate features bunched up with suspicion. "Are you okay?"

"I'm great. Everything's just great."

Her sister handed her a slice of cake. Alexa ignored the dainty dessert fork and scooped up the piece with her hand and shoved it in her mouth.

"It's good, right?"

"Mmm-hmm." She couldn't taste a thing. She might as well have been chewing on a kitchen sponge.

"It's Dev's favorite."

"Tell him he's got good taste."

"Is something wrong? You're a little off."

"I'm fine, Caitlyn," Alexa said wearily. "Please, just drop it."

"I won't just drop it!" Caitlyn insisted. "Something *is* wrong. Now talk!"

"He's upset."

"Who is? Jackson?"

"Who else?"

"Do you know why?"

"Not really."

Alexa licked frosting off her thumb. Caitlyn cut her a sharp look, which could only be interpreted one way: *Quit playing around.*

"He thinks I'm holding out on him."

"Are you holding out on him?"

"Not really."

"Oh, really?" Caitlyn shook her head. "Seeing how sketchy you've been acting lately, my guess is that you are."

Alexa set her empty plate on the console table next to the flowers Jackson had sent her. She could stuff her mouth, but she couldn't stuff down the truth. "I was fired from the firm. No, wait. Actually, I was asked to submit my resignation. There's a difference, but not much."

Caitlyn screeched. "What?"

Alexa shushed her. "Not a word of this to Mom."

"Of course not! I would never…"

"You two seem as thick as thieves lately."

"Because I'm engaged. It's a magical period that

makes your parents treat you like a unicorn. You ought to try it."

There didn't seem to be much chance of that happening. "Whatever. Just don't tell anyone."

"I can keep a secret, Alexa," Caitlyn said. "Now, tell me what happened. How dare they fire you? You're a good attorney."

"I'm an *excellent* attorney."

Her sister reached out and patted her on the shoulder. "Of course, sweetie." Her voice was syrupy, as if she were trying to placate a difficult child, which wasn't too far from the truth. "What went wrong?"

"It came down to a choice between me and the office golden boy. They picked him."

"Why did they have to choose? And how did it come down to a binary choice?"

"Because we couldn't work together."

"Why not?"

"He was making things…uncomfortable at the office."

"Uncomfortable how?"

Alexa realized that she was using coded language to better tuck away the truth. Better to come out with it. "He was making advances."

"He was *harassing* you."

"Yes…that."

Caitlyn's grip on the extra plate of cake tightened until her knuckles turned white. She picked up the dessert fork and stuffed cake in her mouth.

"I filed a complaint," Alexa continued. "Nothing came of it."

"Naturally."

"He's involved with one of the partners' daughter, so there's that."

"Go on."

"He got a slap on the wrist. I was advised to take some time for myself, just until things cooled down. It worked out great because I was needed here. Now they're using my extended absence as an excuse to get rid of me."

"You were gone for just a few weeks!"

"They say my commitment to the firm is in question."

"You're gonna fight back, right?" Caitlyn said between bites of cake. "I mean…you're gonna do *something*."

"I'm going to put all this business behind me. That's what I'm going to do."

"Is that why Jackson is upset? Because you don't want to fight back?"

"No. That's not it."

Something moved inside Alexa. She and Jackson hadn't even made it that far, but she suspected that it would be an issue when they got there.

"Well, I'm upset!" Caitlyn said. "Women have to speak up. You of all people should know that."

"And I know how disruptive litigation can be. They'll never settle. They'll drag this out in court just to soil my reputation."

"You don't know that," Caitlyn said. "Call their bluff."

It was all well and good for her to say that, but it was Alexa's professional reputation that was on the line.

Caitlyn had finished the cake in a few bites. "When Dad finds out… Whew!"

"He can't find out! No one can find out."

"I knew something was up with you, but I thought you were lonely or just tired of being single. Then Jackson comes along, and you still had that look in your eyes."

"What look?"

"The look of someone who needs help. It was obvious something was chipping away at your self-confidence."

"Nothing was chipping away at anything," Alexa said hotly. "I had it under control."

"I can see that."

"And for the record, I wasn't lonely."

"Uh-huh."

"This is why I haven't told Jackson! I knew he'd react like this."

"You haven't told Jackson *any* of this?"

Alexa stepped back. "Not yet."

"What are you waiting for?"

"Just wanted to sort things out."

"All that time you two were at the cabin, what were you talking about?"

"Things."

"God... Alexa!" Caitlyn shook her head. "No wonder he's upset."

"I didn't want to burden him."

"That's how relationships work," she said. "Look it up. I'm sure there's a Harvard lecture series on the topic."

Alexa fiddled with the miniature queen pendant. "I know how relationships work."

"Sorry, you don't," Caitlyn said. "You gloss over everything with a perfect filter. You do it with me, with him, with everyone."

"I do not." The words barely squeaked past her throat. It was true that she had never let go of her alter ego, Alexandra the First.

"Just talk to him. He's probably imagining the worst."

Defeated, Alexa agreed. "I'll talk to him tonight."

"There's my brave big sister!" Caitlyn pinched her cheek. "Now, I've got to head back. I shouldn't leave Dev alone in the lion's den."

Alexa had no time to waste. She was still haunted by the look Jackson had tossed her on his way out the door. Something was broken between them, and it was up to her to fix it. Caitlyn was right. He suspected she was holding back. Who knew what he was thinking? He was likely imagining the worst.

The funny thing was, she'd only made it through this ordeal because of him. His queen chess piece pendant had worked like a charm to keep her calm and composed even during the most contentious meeting of her life. Knowing that he was waiting for her here, at home, had weakened the blow of getting sacked. Leaving Miami had been the easiest decision of her life. With so much to look forward to, she was running toward her future, not away from her past. That evening, when she knocked on his door, she vowed to clear up any misunderstandings and put their relationship back on track.

Jackson opened the door. No shirt, no tie —no pants, even. He wore a towel wrapped low on his hips. Her well-rehearsed script was erased from her mind.

"Do you always answer the door like this?"

"I just got back from work and was about to jump into the shower," he explained.

"I could have been anyone."

Oh, great. Having lost her words, she'd stolen Barbara Lattimore's material. What was she going to do next? Correct his grammar?

"I knew it was you," he said. "And you're not just *anyone*."

Alexa followed him into the main room, noting his stiff posture. The tension between them had not dissipated, and she had not helped her cause just now.

She caught him by the arm. He could at least look at her. "I know I've been withdrawn these last few days, but why are you so upset?"

"Alexa, it's more than that."

"I know…"

She rushed to him and buried her face in his chest. His skin was warm. He stiffened for an instant, but only for an instant. The next moment, his hands were in her hair and their kiss went deep. They'd only been apart a couple of days, and yet she craved his touch and missed his kiss. His muscles were taut, and they tensed under her touch. When she tried to loosen the towel, he broke the kiss and searched her eyes.

Alexa started to tear up. "I'm not just anyone."

The words had slipped out in a breath. She was desperate to remind him of what they had. It was a rare connection that spanned years. Nothing she'd done was so terrible that it should jeopardize that.

"You're the woman who's going to do me in."

"That's not true!" she cried, her heart slamming in her chest. "I'm the woman who loves you."

"Alexa…" He drew her to him and kissed her breathless.

Jackson broke away again. His expression was as serious as she'd ever seen it, but there was a glint in his eyes. They'd started as opponents and would likely match wits to the very end. She wouldn't have it any other way.

"We're not in high school," he said. "You have to learn to trust me."

"I trust you!"

"No, you don't," he said. "We're adults. If we're going to be together, we have to communicate."

Alexa nodded. Communication was crucial, vital, but now wasn't the time.

"Make love to me first."

He swore, but then swooped her up and carried her into the bedroom. They made love in slow, rhythmic circles until pleasure swirled inside her, blinded her. He held her trembling body until she calmed down, stroking her back, kissing her eyelids and calling her "my love." Alexa clung to him. If she had to lose everything that she'd worked so hard for just to get to this place, it would have been well worth it.

Much later, Alexa paced the bathroom's marble floor and marveled that it was heated. She wiggled her toes. "So warm and cozy. Are the towel racks heated?"

"Yes, they are."

"Fancy."

"You can thank my interior designer."

Jackson was finally getting around to that shower, and she was joining him. He switched on the water and beckoned her. "Come," he said. "It's warm and cozy in here."

Alexa quickly removed her gold earrings and watch.

They were valuable vintage pieces, handed down by her grandmother. To this small pile, she added the gold necklace with the queen pendent. It was valuable, too.

He welcomed her in the shower with a sloppy kiss and slid his wet lips down her neck. She smoothed her palms over his short hair beading with water. If there ever was a place to come clean, this was it.

She held his face between her hands. "I have so many things to tell you. I don't know where to start."

Jackson inched back, brows furrowed. "Start anywhere. I'll make sense of it."

"It doesn't make sense to me." The water stung her eyes now. "I got fired. Can you believe it? *Me*. Fired!"

"All right."

"I didn't do anything wrong," she added hastily. "I *hustled* for those people. Brought in clients. Won cases. Networked like crazy. I did all that and they still chose someone else over me."

"Maybe now it's time to hustle for yourself."

"I knew you were going to say that."

"Well…you know me."

"It's easy to build from success. It's a whole other thing to start from ashes. Failure follows you."

"Babe…it doesn't work like that. I promise it doesn't. Just tell me what happened."

Alexa tried her best to link the events in chronological order in her mind. "I've been up nights just trying—"

Jackson tightened his embrace. "Baby, it's okay."

"I failed at the one thing I devoted my life to. That's *not* okay."

"Darling…" He swept back her damp hair. "Walk me through it. We'll sort it out."

Alexa took a breath and began. She poured out her secrets, wishing each revelation would swirl down the drain and disappear. She told him everything: Theo Redmond and the whole mess at A & C. How she'd been forced out, despite having done her best work for them. How lost she felt now even though, deep down, she was relieved to be free and excited to explore her prospects. She shared her dreams, the ones she hadn't dared articulate: moving back to Royal, for good this time, and starting her own firm. She admitted that all her dreams swirled around him and that he had, in some way, guided her home.

Jackson listened, wiped the tears that had mingled with the shower water, kissed her when she hesitated and did not say a word until she asked him what he was thinking. "You need to sue," he said. "Take them to court."

Oh, God, here we go… "I want to look forward, not backwards."

"You want to avoid conflict."

He had it wrong. She was a litigator. Conflict was her bread and butter. But a lawyer was not supposed to be the plaintiff and victim. It would make her look weak. Plus, she wasn't naive. These sorts of complaints were more often than not settled out of court. She didn't want or need A & C's money. "There's more to it than that. They'll fight, drag it out forever and trash my reputation. The most I'll get out of it is a cash settlement."

"Alexa…" He caught her chin with wet, rough hands. Fragrant steam from the shower thickened around them, a buffer from the world. "They're already trashing your reputation."

"That's not true." That day in Arthur's office, they had come to an agreement.

"Yes, it is."

"How do you know?"

How *could* he possibly know? She'd only just told him about the whole ordeal two seconds ago.

"I wasn't going to tell you this, but here goes."

As it turned out, Jackson had secrets of his own. Those damn roses! A quick call to her office to verify the delivery address had ended with shocking revelations. Sweet-as-cake Patty had *trashed* her. Alexa closed her eyes. Fat drops of water pelted her skin, aggravating her frayed nerves.

"You knew all this time?"

"All what time?" he asked. "I came rushing over to you as soon as—"

"You let me carry on as if nothing had happened."

Jackson released her. "Alexa, I gave you every opportunity to open up to me."

The steam was suffocating. She swiveled around and pushed open the shower door. Cool air slapped her face. Jackson cut off the water. His voice was strained when he called after her. "What are you doing?"

"I need fresh air."

She grabbed a towel off the warming rack and rubbed her body with vigor. All the while, shame and mortification blazed through her. Patty had called her a troublemaker to a random stranger who called to inquire about a delivery. Who else was she bad-mouthing her to? The mailman? The sandwich-delivery guy? Had A & C orchestrated a full-on smear campaign? And Jackson knew! All this time, he knew and was feeling... What? Sorry for her? Nausea swirled inside her belly. How could she ever look him in the eye again?

"Darling, don't worry," he said. "I've already returned fire."

Alexa froze, clutching the heavy bath towel to her chest. "What do you mean?"

"A new client of mine mentioned she was meeting with a lawyer from your firm's Dallas office. She thought they had a good reputation. I set her straight. She dropped them and advised two others to do the same. I hope it goes on like this. I'm not going to rest until their reputation is mud."

He stood naked, hands on his hips—dark, dripping, quite obviously unbothered by the cold air. A pity... All she wanted to do was strangle him right now.

"Jackson, stop talking. Every word you say makes me want to scream."

"Mind telling me why?"

"You're intervening...meddling...stirring things up." She was babbling now. Outrage and indignation had short-circuited her brain.

"Or just taking action, which is something you've forgotten how to do."

"Oh, shut up! Don't you dare judge me!"

Jackson let out a low whistle. He grabbed the last remaining towel and wrapped it around his waist. She was back to being someone he had to shield himself from. It hurt, but she couldn't let that distract her. He'd overstepped.

Alexa scurried around, looking for her clothes. She found everything where they'd left them, scattered on the bedroom floor. She quickly dressed and was about to storm out when she remembered her grandmother's watch, gold earrings and the necklace.

Jackson was still in the bathroom, apparently too stunned to move. The nerve of him! He was not the aggrieved party here. His brown eyes were muddied with confusion and pain. The look he gave her tore her in half. She wanted to run to him and run away at the same time. The bathroom was still warm, a reminder of how close they'd been only a moment earlier. Was she kidding herself about Jackson? They couldn't manage to sustain momentum. The glimmer of the queen pendant drew her gaze away. Anger zipped through her again. She grabbed the watch and the earrings off the vanity and stormed out without a word, leaving the necklace behind.

Twenty-Four

Tap! Tap! Tap!

The light knock on her bedroom door grew insistent. Alexa ignored it and sank deeper under her duvet. Unless the house was on fire, she had no intention of budging. It was early, barely seven, and her blackout drapes were sealed shut. Even if she hadn't spent most of the night crying, she still wouldn't be open for business. Her mother—and it could only be her mother—would have to learn to respect her boundaries.

A voice broke through. "Hey! Are you in there? It's me!"

Alexa peered out from under the duvet. "Caitlyn?"

The door creaked open. Her sister popped her head through the crack. "Morning, sunshine! May I come in?"

"Does it make a difference what I say?"

"Nope."

Her mother wasn't the only one who would have to learn boundaries. Alexa waved her in. Caitlyn redeemed herself with coffee, a mug in each hand. She pushed the door shut with her foot.

Dressed for work in a light blazer and jeans, Caitlyn was far more chipper than anyone had the right to be. Her career was on track. She had worked as the ranch's office manager since graduating from college. Recently, she'd started a horseback riding program for foster children at the ranch Dev bought. She was quiet and understated yet focused and determined. Alexa could take some career tips from her little sister.

Caitlyn set one of the mugs on the bedside table, right next to the bouquet of roses. Her mother had had it sent up to her room yesterday afternoon. Now the blood-red blooms served only to remind her of the tragic end of her affair.

"I brought coffee, but I have to get to work soon," Caitlyn proclaimed as she moved about the room, opening the curtains. "Now, spill it! How did it go with Jackson last night?"

Seduced by the aroma of freshly brewed coffee, Alexa sat up in bed and reached for the cup. Her sister took in her appearance and froze. "Whoa, Medusa! What happened to you?"

"I don't want to talk about it."

Alexa had tumbled into bed last night, her hair still damp and tangled from the shower. By the feel of things, she was wearing a mop. She sipped her coffee. It needed sugar.

"Want to talk about what happened with Jackson? I expected you to be at his place and was surprised to see your car in the garage."

"Don't you have your own ranch to run? Why are you here so early?"

"I'm stealing a ranch hand for the day. Dad is actually okay with it. Surprised the heck out of me. Now, quit stalling and come out with it," Caitlyn replied.

"And I wish I could paint you a rosy picture, but I can't. Things went from bad to worse."

Caitlyn sat on the corner of the bed, a look of clear exasperation on her face. "How is that possible?"

"Don't do that," Alexa said.

"Do what?"

"Look at me as if I'm to blame, because I'm not."

But you are! her inner voice declared. That voice hadn't shut up once through the night. *This is your fault. Had you been straight with him, you could have spared yourself a ton of grief.*

"Tell me everything," Caitlyn said. "But keep it short. I'll be late for the new kids arriving today."

"Fine! Long story short—Jackson called my office to arrange to have these stupid flowers delivered. The receptionist told him I no longer worked there. When he asked why, she called me a troublemaker and tried to refer him to another attorney. So, in brief, Jackson knew all along that I was holding out on him."

More like, he knew she had lied to his face.

Caitlyn opened round brown eyes. "Yikes! And then what happened?"

"Of course, we had a big fight."

"Why 'of course'? Couldn't you have talked about it? I'm trying to get you two to a space where you use your words to work out conflict."

"Save your efforts," Alexa said. "We had a huge fight...in the shower...which explains my hair."

Caitlyn winked. "A little shower action. I like it!"

"Please, don't."

Alexa set down her coffee mug. She needed both hands to rant like a lunatic. "You're not going to believe what he told me next."

"Go on!"

"He told his client not to do business with A & C because they were mean to his girlfriend. Can you believe that?"

"Honestly? No," Caitlyn replied. "I doubt very much he used those words."

"Okay. I don't know the exact words, but he said something to that effect."

"In his defense, Counselor, it's not like your coworkers forgot your birthday or stole your snacks from the company fridge. They harassed you and treated you unjustly."

"Don't you think I know that?" Alexa cried. "But Jackson's out there trying to singlehandedly destroy the reputation of a well-established law firm."

"He won't have to go it alone for long," Caitlyn said. "I'm ready to join the crusade. I'll order some T-shirts and make signs."

"He overstepped," Alexa snapped. "And I knew this would happen. I *knew* it! Why do you think I didn't tell him? These Royal men are all the same."

"That's not fair. Dev is not like that."

"Dev isn't from here. He grew up on the East Coast."

"My point is—"

"*My* point is, I was right."

"Great! Now, give yourself a gold medal and get past it. There are more important things than being right."

Sure... But none were so satisfying.

"Can you imagine calling an office—or anyplace, really—asking to speak with a friend, someone you know, and getting that sort of response?"

The answer was quite simple: No. It was as rude as rude could get. It was low down and dirty. It was terrible, and she hadn't deserved it.

"After that experience, would you go around recommending that business to your colleagues? Would you do it if the roles were reversed?"

The answer to that was also quite simple.

Caitlyn stood to retrieve a hairbrush and fastener on the vanity. "Sorry. I have to do this. Your hair is driving me crazy."

Her sister brushed her hair into a neat ponytail, all the while doling out standard-issue advice. "Don't give up. Try again. Give him a chance to explain."

Alexa allowed herself to be groomed. It was oddly soothing. Feeling calmer now, her sadness returned. "He says I don't trust him."

"You probably don't," Caitlyn replied. "Let's face it—you have trust issues."

"I had some issues with this particular matter. I don't have trust issues in general."

"You don't trust Grandpa Gus," Caitlyn said.

"That's a bold statement."

"You think he intentionally handed off our oil rights."

Alexa let her silence speak for her. She did believe that, and it had nothing to do with any so-called "trust issues." She'd studied the evidence, and that was where it led. It was time her family faced that fact.

"We'll take this up in our next session," Caitlyn said. "I've got to get to work. I promise to check on you later."

"Okay," Alexa said. "Love you."

Caitlyn dropped the hairbrush. It clattered onto the floor. To Alexa's horror, Caitlyn dove onto the bed, tackled her and trapped her in a hug. Alexa froze before nestling into her sister's embrace. A minute later, though, she wiggled herself free and clobbered Caitlyn with one of the many decorative pillows her mother had piled onto her bed, for no other reason than to prove that she hadn't gone soft.

Just minutes after Caitlyn left, another knock on her bedroom door shredded any hope Alexa had of ever falling back to sleep. And with that hope, she lost any chance of showing up later at Jackson's door looking sane and serene. No matter what the future held for them, she was deeply embarrassed for storming out of his home like a petulant child. She'd left the man standing naked in his bathroom. Even prima donnas had their limits, and she'd exceeded hers.

Another knock, sharper this time, shattered her thoughts. First thing, she was going to order a do-not-disturb sign for her door.

"Come in!" she cried.

The door swung open, and Jackson entered her bedroom. Alexa dug her nails into the palm of her hand to ensure she wasn't dreaming. Impeccably dressed in a tailored herringbone suit and impeccably groomed, he looked as if he'd walked off a film set. Who let him in? Who let him up? Her family home was a fortress. They were a hospitable bunch, but people didn't just wander in and roam the halls. Her mother wouldn't have that. But there he was, striding into her childhood bedroom—which, for some reason had never looked frillier, with its fringed drapes and not-so-shabby-chic furniture. He stopped at the foot of her bed, hands in his pockets. "Hope this isn't a bad time."

Alexa couldn't think of a worse time. She looked a mess. Caitlyn had fastened her hair in a pouf on top of her head. She didn't need a mirror to confirm that her eyes were bloodshot and her face was puffy with sleep deprivation. Plus, he'd robbed her of the chance to show up at his door looking semi-decent, and she was a little salty about it.

"How did you find my room?" she asked.

"Caitlyn let me in and showed me the way."

"Ah." That explained it. "Why are you here? Shouldn't you be at work?"

"A couple of things," he said. "First, I'm here to offer you the opportunity to grovel and make things right."

Alexa let out a soundless laugh. Now *that* was rich.

"I figured you'd avoid me for a month before coming around to it," he continued. "But I don't have that kind of time."

Maybe it was the matter-of-fact delivery or the hidden challenge in his words, but Alexa was awake...and aroused. Jackson Strom knew how to push her every button, and it was nothing less than thrilling.

"Shows how much you know," she said. "I was going to get dressed, put on makeup and show up at your door later today."

He nodded. "Very well. I saved you the trouble."

She propped herself up on her elbows. He claimed to have two items on his agenda. She wanted to hear it. "What's the second reason?"

He met her eyes. "I came to tell you that I love you."

Warmth spread throughout her body and filled her heart. Jackson Strom loved her. He loved her, and that love was going to hold her steady even when life got incredibly rocky.

"Last night I said a lot of things, except that," he went on. "I'm in love with you, Alexa."

"I love you, too, Jackson."

"All right," he said, his tone gentle. "That settles it."

Alexa fell back onto her stack of pillows, but it felt as if she were falling from the sky.

"Don't get too relaxed. We still have unfinished business."

"You mean item number one on your agenda?"

"Yes, of course."

"Are you kidding me?"

"Alexa, I'm in no mood to kid."

She sat up again and crossed her legs. "Is there any particular way you'd like this to go? Any specific language you'd like to hear?"

He folded his arms across his chest. In her dainty bedroom, he looked solid and strong. "Start by saying sorry."

"I *am* sorry, Jackson. I should not have stormed out the way I had."

Jackson tilted his head, considering her words. "Is that all?"

"What else?"

"Can't help you," he said. "You'll have to puzzle this one out."

She grabbed the same frilly pillow she'd clobbered Caitlyn with a moment ago and hugged it to her chest. "I'm sorry I wasn't completely honest with you. Okay?"

He remained impassive. "You'll have to expand on that."

"It's not that I don't trust you, because I do. With my

whole heart, I trust you." Caitlyn's words were bouncing in her head. She had to make that point clear. "I was concerned about how you would react, but mostly I thought I could resolve my issues on my own and leave you out of it."

Jackson was waiting for more, but she couldn't think of anything else to say. Finally, he filled the gap. "You didn't want me to see you fail."

"Can you blame me?" Alexa cried. "We competed as kids, and I always came out on top. But look at us now. My career is in serious jeopardy, and you… Well, you're winning."

He leaned forward and gripped the iron rail of the footboard. "What good is it if I lose you again?"

"Oh, God." She pressed a palm to her forehead. This man was going to break her open, and there was nothing she could do about it.

Jackson straightened up, stripped off his suit jacket and tossed it onto the window bench. He then hunched low to unlace his polished leather shoes.

"What are you doing?" she asked.

He didn't answer. Instead, he joined her on the bed and gathered her in his arms. The old bedframe creaked. Alexa momentarily forgot they were midargument. She nestled closer to him and breathed in the clean scent of his skin. Yesterday, she'd walked away from this. She must not have been in her right mind.

The bed squeaked again. Jackson reached overhead and shook the vintage wrought iron headboard. "What is all this dollhouse furniture?"

"This is my mother's attempt at French provincial decor. She found these pieces at a flea market in Austin. It hasn't been touched since I left for college."

"Oh yeah?" he said. "Where are all of the boy band posters?"

"She stripped those down the day I left."

"How many nights did you spend in here plotting my downfall?"

"Way too many."

"Well, it worked." He kissed her forehead. "I fell for you hard. And I want you in my life. The question is, do you want me?"

She curled a hand around his tie. "Of course I do!"

"It's not that you didn't confide in me," he said. "It's that you didn't even want me to know something was wrong. I kept asking and you dodged the question every time."

"All I wanted was a chance to clean up the mess in Miami before coming back to you."

"That's not how it works," he said.

"How does it work, Jackson?" she asked. "I'm at a loss."

"Just talk to me," he said. "Trust me enough to tell me when you're hurting. I wouldn't have rushed off to fight your battles if that's what you were worried about. I respect you too much."

That had been part of it. Mostly, she had never wanted to be anything less to him than Alexandra the First, the girl whom he had admired at fifteen. Feeling uneasy, she reached for the little gold chess piece at her neck. It wasn't there, and its absence turned her uneasiness into boiling turmoil.

"I want my necklace back," she said. "I miss it."

"In that case..." He reached into the pocket of his trousers and dug out the familiar green velvet pouch. "Here you go, my queen."

Alexa snatched it from him, shook out the gold neck-lace and fastened it around her neck without his help. The pendant slid into the groove at the base of her neck. She traced its shape with her fingertips and sighed. "Much better." She could breathe again and think clearly. "Is this thing magic?"

"If luck is magic," he said. "The day I ran into you at the TCC pool party was the luckiest day of my life. That morning, I wasn't even sure I wanted to go."

Alexa didn't believe in luck. She put her faith in well-mapped plans. "Okay. Here's what we're going to do. You head back to work. I'm going to reach out to a law school friend. She's an attorney who specializes in employment law. I'm going to sue A & C."

His smile stretched into an I-told-you-so smirk. "Let's ruin them."

God, he was sexy when wicked. "I'm only seeking damages for wrongful termination. It won't put a dent in the firm's business, but they'll remember my name."

"I'm down for whatever you want to do."

"I want you to go to work," she said. "I'll come over tonight looking beautiful and rested, and we'll have the night that we should've had."

"I've got a better plan." He rolled on top of her and kissed her until she was winded again. "Let's play hooky."

She wrapped her arms around his neck, excitement rippling through her. "I've never done that."

"I'm not surprised."

"What would we even do? Spend the day playing pool in some kid's rec room?"

"Actually, we'd drive to the next county to shoot darts and drink beer."

Alexa laughed. How was that any better? "Not my style. I think I'll pass."

He tugged at her earlobe with his teeth. "Don't worry. I'll get you home before curfew."

"Jackson," Alexa whispered. "I'd break any rule for you."

He raised his head and looked at her through lowered lashes. Even so, she could see the emotion in his eyes. "We're in love," he whispered. "Wait until I tell our class Facebook group. They voted you most likely to break my heart."

"When did this vote happen?"

"That day we all played hooky."

"Makes sense."

"Maybe I won't take you home in time for curfew," he said. "Maybe I'll keep you."

Alexa went soft with love. There was nothing she wanted more. *Keep me. Keep me forever.* That was what she wanted to say. Instead, she kissed him and murmured against his lips, "I'm going to crush you at darts."

They did not drive to the next county. Instead, they drove out to North Cove Park, found a sturdy oak tree and got busy carving.

A-JACKS 4EVER <3

* * * * *

Don't miss the next installment in
Texas Cattleman's Club: Ranchers and Rivals,
Vacation Crush
by Yahrah St. John.

**WE HOPE YOU ENJOYED
THIS BOOK FROM**

HARLEQUIN
DESIRE

*Luxury, scandal, desire—welcome to
the lives of the American elite.*

Be transported to the worlds of oil barons, family dynasties,
moguls and celebrities. Get ready for juicy plot twists,
delicious sensuality and intriguing scandal.

6 NEW BOOKS AVAILABLE EVERY MONTH!

#2893 VACATION CRUSH
Texas Cattleman's Club: Ranchers and Rivals
by Yahrah St. John
What do you do after confessing a crush on an accidental livestream?
Take a vacation to escape the gossip! But when Natalie Hastings gets to
the resort, her crush—handsome rancher Jonathan Lattimore—is there
too. Will one little vacation fling be enough?

#2894 THE MARRIAGE MANDATE
Dynasties: Tech Tycoons • by Shannon McKenna
Pressured into marrying, heiress Maddie Moss chooses the last man in
the world her family will accept—her brother's ex–business partner,
Jack Daly. Accused of destroying the company, Jack can use the
opportunity to finally prove his innocence—but only if he can resist Maddie...

#2895 A RANCHER'S REWARD
Heirs of Hardwell Ranch • by J. Margot Critch
To earn a large inheritance, playboy rancher Garrett Hardwell needs a
fake fiancée—fast! Wedding planner Willa Statler is the best choice. The
problem? She's his best friend's younger sister! With so much at stake, will
their very real connection ruin everything?

#2896 SECOND CHANCE VOWS
Angel's Share • by Jules Bennett
Despite their undeniable chemistry, Camden Preston and Delilah Hawthorn
are separating. With divorce looming, Delilah is shocked when her blind
date at a masquerade gala turns out to be her husband! The attraction's
still there, but can they overcome what tore them apart?

#2897 BLACK SHEEP BARGAIN
Billionaires of Boston • by Naima Simone
Abandoned at birth, CEO Nico Morgan will upend the one thing his father
loved most—his company. Integral to the plan is a charming partner, and
that's his ex, Athena Evans. But old feelings and hot passion could derail
everything...

#2898 SECRET LIVED AFTER HOURS
The Kane Heirs • by Cynthia St. Aubin
Finding his father's assistant at an underground fight club, playboy
Mason Kane realizes he isn't the only one leading a double life. So he
offers Charlotte Westbrook a whirlwind Riviera fling to help her loosen up,
but it could cost her job and her heart...

"This won't work. You know it won't." Felicity continued. "If the baby is your priority, then you and I can't…"

Can't what?" Wynn smiled mockingly.

"You're taunting me, but I don't know why."

"You don't want to *enjoy* each other while you're here?"

"We had our chance. We didn't make it work. And I'm not one for fooling around just for a few orgasms."

"The old Fliss never said things like that."

"The old *Felicity* was an eighteen-year-old kid."

"You always seemed mature for your age. You had a vision for your future and you made it happen. I'm proud of you."

HDEXP0722R

She gaped at him. "Thank you."

"I'm sorry," he said gruffly. "I shouldn't have kissed you. Let's pretend it never happened. A fresh start, Fliss. Please?"

"Of course. We're both here to honor Shandy and care for her daughter. I don't think we should do anything to mess that up."

"Agreed."

Don't miss what happens next in…
The Comeback Heir
by USA TODAY *bestselling author Janice Maynard.*

Available September 2022 wherever
Harlequin Desire books and ebooks are sold.

Harlequin.com

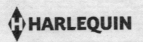

HARLEQUIN

Heartfelt or thrilling, passionate or uplifting—Harlequin is more than just happily-ever-after.

With twelve different series to choose from and new books available every month, you are sure to find stories that will move you, uplift you, inspire and delight you.

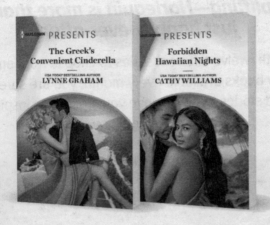